5 —

VAMPIRE ROYALS 3: THE FINALE

LEIGH WALKER

CMG PUBLISHING

CHAPTER 1
ALL THE KING'S MEN

I STARED OUT THE WINDOW AT THE GROUNDS BELOW. The king—tall, muscular, and imposing in his battle uniform—gave a speech in front of his royal army. The Black Guard listened intently. Although I couldn't make out the king's words, I could guess what he was saying.

The rebel army is out there.

We must find them. And kill them.

Take prisoners only if you believe they'll be of use.

He finished his monologue and stood before them, his white beard gleaming in the early morning light. From here, he didn't look like a vampire. But I knew better.

The Black Guard—comprised of all vampire soldiers—rallied around their king. They shouted, waving the royal banners. The king bowed, then climbed up on his horse. He started in the direction of the forest. The Guard followed, a hundred soldiers ready to crush the human rebels in the name of the royal family.

I knew I should be relieved. Neither the prince nor

my brother was out there. One a vampire, one a rebel, both were safe for the moment. The prince was likely meeting with his advisors, and my brother was down in the dungeons—a prisoner, but at least he was alive. Still, my heart twisted as the sentinels wielded their banners, the royal colors of purple, red, and the deepest blue streaking across the grounds.

My father was still out there somewhere. I prayed that he was safe.

I heard a knock at the door, and my head maid, Evangeline, stuck her pretty face into the room. "Ah, you're awake. I'll bring your tea shortly. The film crew is going to want to get in here first thing, so you should go and wash up."

"Right." I nodded. "Thank you, Evangeline."

I sighed as she curtsied and left. *Oh, the bloody film crew.* Of course they were coming. I was a finalist in the Pageant, the nationally televised competition that chronicled the prince, His Royal Highness Dallas Black, as he searched for a bride from the settlements. This was our last week at the palace before the competition wrapped up and the winner was announced. Only four girls were left: Shaye Iman, Tamara Layne, Blake Kensington, and me.

As a finalist, I knew I should get to washing up so I looked semi-decent for the film crew. But I didn't leave the window. I leaned my forehead against the glass, hoping its coolness would quiet the rioting in my brain.

The cameras.

The royals.

The rebels.

The Pageant.

The prince.

My brother, down in the dungeons...

A few minutes passed until I heard another knock on the door. Evangeline bustled in with a tea tray, followed closely by my other maids, Bria and Bettina. Evangeline was tall and fair, while Bria and Bettina were both smaller, petite with dark skin. Identical twins, each had almond-shaped eyes and long ebony hair. To help us tell them apart, Bettina always wore a pink ribbon in her ponytail, and Bria always wore a blue one.

"Miss," Evangeline scolded, "the cameras are right behind us."

I ran for the bathroom before they could come in and film me in my nightgown and my braids.

"Hurry!" Bria made a scooting motion as another knock landed on my door. "Just a minute!" she called to them sweetly while glaring at me.

I hustled inside and closed the door. *Game face, Gwyneth, game face.* I looked at myself in the mirror, disappointed to see that no such thing was in sight. Mussed from sleep, my braids had flyaways sticking up all over my head. My eyes were too bright, wild with adrenaline. A V formed in between my eyebrows, a crease from worrying about the king and his army, my brother in the dungeons, my father—out there somewhere and ill—and the fact that I had one week left to win the prince's favor.

I tried to rub the crease from my face, to no avail.

Bria opened the door a crack and scowled at me. "What on earth are you doing? They're waiting!"

"I'm coming. I just... It's just..."

She nodded encouragingly, feigning patience. "Yes, miss?"

"The king and the Black Guard left a few minutes ago. I'm worried." I didn't bother to get into specifics. Concerned about both my father and Dallas's father, I found the whole thing too convoluted to wade into when the cameras were breathing down my neck.

"You need tea." Bria nodded, sure of herself.

"Tea sounds good."

"Then we'll do your hair and fix you up. But you need to put this on and come out straightaway." She handed me a bright-blue dress. "The royal emissary's waiting, too, along with the camera crew."

"Oh dear." Tariq, the royal emissary, was not my favorite person at the palace. He typically asked me to do things I didn't enjoy, like parade around in high heels and curtsy countless times. And worse.

"Hurry." Bria closed the door, and I hastily pulled on the dress. I smoothed the flyaways and splashed cold water on my face. Straightening, I took a deep breath.

I emerged from the bathroom with a smile. Three cameramen were crammed into my chambers, along with all their equipment and, of course, Tariq. This morning, he wore a dark-silver tunic with slim black pants, his hair shellacked back from his handsome, shrewd face.

"Good morning." I greeted the crew. "Tariq." I curtsied.

He smiled at me, his long eyelashes fluttering. "You're getting much better at that, my lady."

"Thank you. You've certainly had me practicing enough."

"Yes, about that. A word, Miss West." Tariq's smile didn't falter as he got to the point. "We'll be filming you this morning taking a walk around the grounds with His Highness, as well as his mother. The queen has declared herself ready, willing, and able to spend time with each of the remaining contestants. She wants to get to know you better."

Oh bloody hell. "Fantastic." I plastered another smile across my face.

Tariq bowed. "I'll leave you to it. Enjoy your morning." Did I imagine it, or did he smirk as he hustled out?

Bria took me firmly by the shoulders and guided me into a seat. Bettina hauled out the makeup crate, while Evangeline dusted the already-immaculate room and hummed to herself. The cameras filmed us as Bria loosened my braids and Bettina took out a tub of sparkly powder.

I kept the smile on my face, even as my heart thudded in my chest. *The queen.* Oh dear Lord, help me. If there was one person who petrified me, it was my potential future mother-in-law.

"Are you ready for me, miss?" Bettina asked.

I nodded.

"Good." She started applying the powder to my face with her favorite poufy brush. "As you're meeting with the queen *and* His Highness, I'll be sure to make you sparkle."

"Thank you, Bettina."

She smiled kindly. "It's my pleasure."

I felt soothed as they worked, relaxing underneath their capable hands. But then I heard another knock at the door.

"Yes?" Evangeline asked.

A sentinel opened the door. "His Royal Highness, Prince Dallas Black, Crown Prince of the United Royal Settlements, has sent word that he will be waiting for Miss West in the grand foyer in ten minutes."

Evangeline nodded. "Miss West will be right down."

The sentinel bowed, then retreated—and any thoughts I'd had of being soothed or relaxed vanished. I forced myself to forget about the queen. I'd quiver about her later. My heart thudded, but this time in excitement, not dread. *The prince.* Only ten more minutes until I got to see the prince.

I counted down the minutes, barely able to contain myself as the twins fixed my flyaways and made me sparkle. I wished I could speak freely, but the bloody cameras recorded our every move. Finally, the twins finished. They nodded and clucked their approval.

"There you are." Bria smoothed my hair one final time.

"Looking lovely as ever." Bettina dabbed one last touch of gloss to my lips.

I rose, and Evangeline clapped. "You're a vision, miss.

Have a wonderful time with His Highness and the queen."

I grinned at her. "Thank you."

I couldn't wait any longer. With a curtsy to the camera crew, I practically ran from the room, high heels be damned.

CHAPTER 2
AN UPHILL BATTLE

FULLY AWARE OF THE LIMITS OF MY GRACEFULNESS, I stopped running when I reached the stairs. Dallas waited for me below, in the lobby of the grand foyer. I couldn't help staring at his tall and handsome form. I did, however, try to keep my mouth closed, lest I drool all over my dress.

The prince was dashing in his ceremonial uniform. His face—which over the past few weeks had grown familiar, and dear—almost undid me. He had a square jaw, patrician nose, and broad cheekbones. His thick, dark-brown hair was tousled, and his deep-brown eyes radiated intelligence and kindness. The white patina of his skin made him look unearthly, an angel sent to live among mere mortals.

A small, playful smile graced his sensuous lips as he watched me carefully navigate the stairs and breathe a sigh of relief as I reached the bottom. "Miss West." He bowed.

I longed to reach out for him, to bury my face against his powerful chest. But another danged film crew surrounded us.

"Your Highness." I curtsied. He wanted me to call him by his first name, but when the cameras were rolling, we both thought it best to stick to a more formal address.

He held out his arm, and my pulse quickened. He drew me against him, and his scent wafted over me, making my mouth water, a Pavlovian response over which I had zero control.

Dallas looked down at me and smiled. He missed nothing, and I could tell he thoroughly enjoyed the effect he had on me. "Good morning."

I grinned back. "Good morning."

"Did you have your breakfast?"

"I had some tea, Your Highness. I expect I'll have a full breakfast in the common room after our walk."

"I know you're always hungry. I brought you this." He snapped his fingers, and a sentinel appeared with a picnic basket. "Shall we?"

I nodded happily, basking in his thoughtfulness. The prince and food were my two favorite things.

"It's warm enough on the front lawn that we can sit out there and eat before we meet the queen." He cleared his throat. "Tariq informed you about that, correct?"

"Yes." I kept my voice even, refusing to show my nerves. The queen frightened me, but she was Dallas's mother. I had to make an effort not only to be brave but also to be friendly. I just hoped she didn't get displeased and drain me dry.

Sensing my discomfort, Dallas stopped and motioned to the camera crew. "You may film us having breakfast, but keep your distance so that we may have a private conversation."

"Yes, Your Highness." The entire crew nodded. The last time the prince had asked for privacy, they'd ignored him. Dallas had made it clear that was never to happen again, otherwise heads would roll. I had a feeling he didn't usually have to give these sorts of instructions twice.

Two sentinels opened the front doors for us, and we stepped out into the crisp, sunny morning. More sentinels waited on the massive front lawn, where they'd spread a heavy blanket for us to sit. The sun climbed in the sky and warmed my face. I leaned in closer to Dallas, enjoying the moment.

"I've missed you, Gwyneth."

I smiled up at him. It had been only a day since the royal gala, but Dallas had been in meetings, and I hadn't seen him. Only a day, but it felt like forever. "I've missed you, too."

We reached the blanket, and the sentinels bowed. One handed Dallas a shawl, which he carefully wrapped around my shoulders. I was touched by his thoughtfulness. "Thank you."

"It's my pleasure." He nodded to the soldiers, and they retreated, joining the camera crew at the front of the palace, a respectable distance away from us.

The sun glinted against the facade of the castle, warming its gray stones. Its imposing beauty took my breath away.

"What are you thinking?" Dallas asked.

"Just that the castle is lovely. And a bit overwhelming."

He watched my face. "I've found ways to make it a home. The winter garden, my chambers, the stables— these are the places I return to when it all seems too much. Our northern compound was much smaller than this. It was an adjustment at first, to be sure. It gets...easier."

"What's it like? Up north?"

A shadow fell across his face. "It used to be beautiful. But outside influences have brought its ruin. It's hardly habitable anymore."

"What sort of outside influences? And what about your brother? Is he safe?" Dallas had told me his younger brother refused to leave their family home.

"I expect Austin will be here soon enough. Mother and father have ordered him to come down for the final portion of the show."

"You mean for the engagement?"

"Yes." Dallas coughed, and did I imagine it, or did he blush? "As for the outside influences that infiltrated the North, please believe me when I tell you—you don't want to know."

I put my hands on my hips. "I beg your pardon, but I absolutely want to know. Is this about the werewolves?"

He'd mentioned werewolves several times and never in a nice way.

"Gwyneth, enough about that. How about some tea?" He smiled at me in a manner that indicated the subject was closed.

We both sat down, and I wrapped the shawl around me. Dallas poured tea from a thermos, then brought out a tin of scones—raspberry, blueberry, and blackberry. Now my mouth watered for an entirely different reason. "Ooh, you brought scones. Thank you."

He grinned as he spread butter onto the blackberry one and handed it to me. "I know you enjoy them."

I took a bite and moaned. "Whatever you're paying your kitchen staff, it's not enough."

He chuckled, then his expression turned serious. "We have quite a few things to discuss before my mother joins us."

"Like the werewolves?"

He blinked. "No. Not the bloody werewolves."

"Oh, fine." I'd find another way to learn out about the things he'd mentioned, the werewolves and the gnomes and the problems up north. My gaze flicked to the camera crew. "I suspect they've been following you nonstop since the gala, same as me and the other girls. So you're right. We should talk while we have the chance."

Dallas nodded, the sun dappling his pale skin. I tried not to notice so I could actually talk, not just ogle. "I saw your father this morning, and the Black Guard. It must be difficult for you to have them gone."

The muscle in his jaw tightened. "My father would not listen when I asked him to wait. I don't believe the rebels are close, not after what just happened."

A few weeks ago, a rebel faction had kidnapped me and brought me to their nearby camp. Dallas had tried to free me, but they'd captured him and chained him in silver. The rebels—including my brother—had hoped to kill the prince and attack the palace. But my vampire friend, Eve, had come to our rescue. In the process, she'd slaughtered the rebels at the camp. That was how Balkyn had become a prisoner at the palace—he'd been captured during the battle.

"How long will the king be gone?" I asked.

"It's a day trip, a search mission to make sure the area is clear of any rebel activity."

"Speaking of rebels, how is Balkyn? Have you had word?" My brother had made it clear he wanted nothing to do with me. Per his request, I hadn't visited him, but I hadn't stopped thinking about him.

"He isn't...he isn't doing well, Gwyneth."

My heart lurched. "What's happened?"

The prince pulled up a blade of grass and examined it. "He is refusing to eat, I'm afraid."

I put down my scone, feeling sick. "I have to do something. I'll go and see him."

Dallas frowned, his eyes stormy. "Do you think it will help?"

"I don't know, but I have to try. Does the king know yet? That Balkyn is my brother?"

"No. I have kept that to myself for now. My father's on the warpath. He wants the contest wrapped up and plans for the wedding finalized—he wants to go on the offensive against the rebels. And I'm worried that he won't take the news well, even though I want him to know the truth."

I nodded, my eyes filling with tears. Dallas was risking himself to protect me. "Thank you."

"Don't thank me. I have your brother locked in the dungeons. I'm hardly your knight in shining armor now."

"That's not true. You saved me, and you spared his life." I wiped at my eyes, trying to keep my makeup intact. "May I please see him? Without you getting into trouble?"

"Yes." But Dallas didn't look happy about it. "I'll arrange for you to go as soon as possible, with full security. But I want to be at the castle when you visit, just in case..."

"In case what?"

He reached for my hand. "In case you need me."

"That's very kind, but he *is* my brother. I can handle him."

A dark look crossed the prince's handsome face, as if he'd tasted something bitter. "He was unkind to you, Gwyneth. I would prefer to be here."

My heart twisted. Dallas thought he had to protect me from my own brother, who I loved but who had become a stranger to me over the past five years. "I understand." I wished I didn't.

"On to the next unpleasant topic." The camera crew kept filming. Dallas ignored them, his gaze locked with mine. "I'm going to Settlement Eleven with Tamara this afternoon."

"Of course." My stomach plummeted, but I tried to keep my distaste from showing on my face. Tamara was attractive, wealthy, and from a good family that supported the royals. She was Tariq's favorite, so I wasn't surprised that her visit was scheduled first.

"When I return, I'll have meetings with my staff and advisors. I'll make sure the arrangements are made for you to see Balkyn during that time. But then I'm going to the next settlement visit straightaway. I don't know which one. They're working on the production schedule at the moment."

I nodded. "This is all happening so fast."

Dallas raked a hand through his hair, making it a bit wild. "Will you be okay while I'm gone? I'll make sure you have plenty of guards and are safe, but..." He looked miserable as his voice trailed off.

I lifted my chin. "I'll be fine. I have more important things to worry about than Tamara."

He winced. "Speaking of which, we should get going. Mother will be waiting."

I nodded, praying my game face was intact.

Dallas helped me to my feet. "You don't have to be afraid of my mother, Gwyneth."

So much for my game face.

"No harm will come to you, I swear it. I've been

working with her. So has Eve. We're trying to bring her into this century so she understands her old ways of... responding...to things are no longer appropriate."

The queen's old way of "responding" to things was to sink her fangs into anyone who offended her. Which was how my friend Eve had become a vampire—the queen herself had turned her.

"She really wants to get to know you."

I forced myself to smile. "That's very kind." I was still scared of her, though.

"No one said this was going to be easy." Dallas reached for my hand. He raised it to his lips and kissed it. "We *are* vampire and human, after all. We're intrinsically complicated." He pulled me to my feet.

"How so?"

He brushed the hair back from my forehead, his face inches from mine, and I cursed the cameras. "Because you smell mouthwatering to me. And my mother drained your friend dry and turned her. And your brother is locked in my dungeon and wants me dead. That's just to name a few complications."

"None of that matters." I clasped his hands. "Balkyn doesn't know you. He doesn't understand that you've saved my life, more than once. And Eve is getting on all right." In fact, my friend had told me she loved being a vampire.

I looked up at Dallas, wishing I were brave enough to say what I really felt. *None of it matters, because I could never live without you.*

Instead, I lightened my tone and put on another

smile. "As for being mouthwatering, I understand it's quite the compliment. And frankly, I wouldn't have it any other way."

He chuckled, and my insides twisted with longing. "Nor would I, Gwyneth. Nor would I."

CHAPTER 3
NEVER BREAK THE CHAIN

I'D SAID I WAS SCARED OF THE QUEEN, BUT I MEANT that I was petrified. Waiting outside the entrance to the palace for her arrival, I longed to flee. The camera crew set up on the lawn, eagerly awaiting the queen's entrance. The people in the settlements viewed Her Majesty as exotic and mysterious. Her interactions with the remaining contestants would make for excellent television.

Finally, the doors opened, and Dallas's mother swept through.

"Her Royal Majesty, Queen Serena Black, Crown Queen of the United Royal Settlements," a sentinel announced.

All of the guards bowed before Her Highness. She descended the steps slowly, deliberately, and I was forced to confront her icy beauty in broad daylight. Tall and slender, with sapphire-blue eyes, she was stunning. Her pale complexion was set off by a sumptuous black gown.

In the light, her skin was so white, it was as if she'd never been in the sun before.

I suddenly squeezed Dallas's hand. "Wait—the sun! Is it safe for her to be out in the daylight?"

"Yes, of course." Dallas pulled me closer, clearly sensing that my nerves were about to get the better of me. "Just not for too long. This is new for her, actually. She prefers to stay in her chambers during the day, but she's really making an effort."

"That's w-wonderful." I hoped the sun didn't make her cranky.

The queen reached us. Dallas bowed, and I curtsied.

He smiled and took her hand. "Mother. You remember Miss Gwyneth West, from Settlement Four."

The queen's glittering blue gaze raked over me. "Yes. It's a pleasure to see you." Her words were stiff, as if she was out of practice exchanging small pleasantries.

"The pleasure is mine, Your Majesty." I smiled at her tentatively.

She did not smile back but nodded instead. Then she accepted the arm Dallas offered.

"We'll walk around to the reflecting pools if that's acceptable to you, Mother." His tone was filled with kindness, and I melted toward him even more.

She nodded again, and this time it seemed more natural. "That would be nice." She surveyed the grounds. "It's been a long time since I've been outside during the day. It's quite different. A bit jarring, I think, all this brightness."

Dallas tilted his chin up. "The sun feels nice on your face, though, once you get used to it."

The queen lifted her chin, too, closing her eyes briefly. "You're right."

He chuckled. "Of course, Mother—I'm always right."

Her eyes snapped open. "You and your brother. Ridiculous egos." She chuckled.

I fought to keep my jaw from dropping. The queen could *chuckle*?

Keeping an arm linked through his mother's, Dallas reached for me with his free hand. He twined his fingers through mine, and the three of us strolled forward. It was an odd feeling, being linked to both of them like that.

"Mother, Gwyneth's an accomplished rider. She loves visiting the horses in the stables."

"Really?" The queen peered across her son's broad chest. "Which horse is your favorite?"

I cleared my throat. "M-Maeve, Your Highness. One of the white mares."

"Ah, yes. She's a beauty." Her gaze traveled over to her son's face. "So you two can enjoy that together."

"Yes, Mother."

The queen nodded. "It's important to have things in common. Particularly when you're not of the same race."

"Mother." Dallas raised his eyebrows. "What have I told you? Our different backgrounds don't matter."

She stopped walking. "Did they matter when you went to rescue her and the human rebels tried to kill you because you're a vampire?"

Dallas regarded her. "I see Father has kept you up to date."

The queen arched an eyebrow. "We are running this country together, you know. Secrets won't do."

A chill needled my spine as I thought about my brother, locked away in the dungeons. *Talk about secrets.*

"Mother... How can I make you understand? Our different backgrounds don't matter to me, and my counsel is the only one I plan to keep. Gwyneth and I care about the same things. That's what matters to me."

She looked past him to me. "Gwyneth?"

My insides went all spongy and weird when she said my name. "Yes, Your Majesty?"

"What sorts of things do you care about?"

"Well, I care about my family. I love them very much." *Don't blather on,* I warned myself, *and for the love of all things holy, don't mention your brother, the rebel prisoner!* "As I'm sure you know, my younger brother and sister live at home with my mother in Settlement Four. We're very close."

"I watched the episode when you went home. They are quite cute."

"Thank you, Your Majesty." I was flabbergasted. "Cute" wasn't a word I ever expected to hear from the queen. She'd certainly surprised me today.

"And do you take care of them, when you are home?" she asked.

"Yes."

"And what will happen if my son chooses you to be his bride? Will your family move here?"

"Uh. I..." I looked to Dallas, completely baffled.

He stared straight ahead. Again, I swore he was blushing.

"I suppose my family would do whatever the royal family is most comfortable with, in addition to what they feel is best for them." I cleared my throat. "To be honest, I hadn't considered it yet, Your Majesty. The contest has been quite all-encompassing."

We rounded the castle, and the queen gazed at the reflecting pool. "But you must consider it. I know my son would like to pretend that humans and vampires are one big happy family, but I would not be so simplistic with respect to such matters."

Dallas shook his head. "I'm not being simplistic, Mother. I'm being optimistic. Forward-thinking. There's no reason humans and vampires can't live together in harmony. Think of all the human servants who live and work at the palace."

The queen pointed at me. "Think of this girl's friend —Eve—and what I did to her the first night she got here."

She stepped away, staring at the water in the pool, a dark look crossing her snow-white face.

"We've discussed that. I understand why you did it." Dallas's voice was tender. "You're working on your issues."

"Issues?" The queen scoffed. "If you call drinking human blood an issue, well...I am afraid you are setting yourself up for a grave disappointment in the future. It's not as though we can change our very nature."

Dallas sighed. "That's not what I meant. I don't expect that our kind will stop drinking blood. That is how we survive. I was talking about the fact that she insulted you, and you couldn't control your rage."

The queen's gaze flicked to me. "You're getting quite an earful this morning, aren't you?"

I cleared my throat. "Yes, Your Majesty. But I want to hear it. And as for Eve..." My voice trailed off, and I looked to both of them, unsure whether to proceed.

"Yes? What about her?" The queen's eyes glittered with curiosity.

Dallas nodded, and I continued. "She's very sorry about what she said to you. She sees it differently now. She views her new life as a gift from fate. An opportunity to see both sides whereas, before, she only viewed vampires through her own bias. She's quite extraordinary, actually."

The queen tilted her chin, inspecting me. "Yes she is. And I wonder if she wasn't correct about it being fate that brought her here to the castle."

"You believe in fate?"

Her gaze traveled to her son. "I do."

An emotion briefly crossed Dallas's face, but I wasn't quick enough to read it. He rearranged his features and smiled, holding out his arms for both of us. "Come now. We're getting awfully philosophical for first thing in the morning."

My head was spinning by the time I got to the common room. The queen's question about where my mother, Remy, and Winnie would live had caught me wholly off guard. Delicious breakfast smells wafted to me, but I couldn't concentrate on them.

Suddenly, the fact that the contest had only one week left seemed very real. I was woefully unprepared for that. Questions I couldn't begin to answer swirled through my mind.

What if Dallas chooses someone else?

What if he...doesn't?

"Well, there she is. Little Miss First and Foremost." Tamara frowned at me from the table where she sat with Blake and Shaye.

Here we go. I headed for them, my remaining fellow contestants, and prepared myself for a ribbing. The three of them watched me as I crossed the room: Miss Tamara Layne, Settlement 11, with her long dark hair and blue eyes framed by thick lashes; Miss Shaye Iman, Settlement 24, with thick, tawny ringlets, enormous brown eyes, and copper-colored skin; and Miss Blake Kensington, Settlement 15, with long, thick blond hair, a gorgeous face, and the ability to out-eat us all.

"I beg your pardon?" I sank into my chair, scowling at Tamara. "Little Miss What?"

Tamara tossed her raven waves over her shoulder and inspected me. "We were just discussing how you always seem to get the prince's attention first and how none of us can figure out *why*."

"That's not what we were saying, you insipid cow."

Blake pinged her toast crust onto Tamara's plate. "*You* were complaining that Gwyneth always gets the prince's attention first, and then you were listing all of your so-called superior assets. Shaye and I were just sitting here, gritting our teeth."

I chuckled, looking from Blake to Shaye. "Thank you."

Tamara rolled her eyes. "My assets are superior, though. Which is why I find it so vexing that His Highness took you for a walk with the queen this morning— and not me."

"Oh, do tell us." Shaye leaned forward, her curls glistening in the sun streaming in through the windows. "How was she?"

"She was...good. It was nice, actually."

"You and your 'nice.'" Tamara yawned dramatically. "I've just got up, and here you are putting me to sleep again."

"What's the queen like?" Shaye asked. "Whenever we've seen her, she's been imposing. And a bit terrifying, if I'm being honest."

I nodded. "She's definitely old school. Old *vampire* school, which is a whole other category. But she came out in the sun today because she wants to make an effort. She wants to get to know each one of us. She was quite pleasant, actually."

"Hmm. I've no idea what I'm going to talk to her about." Blake fiddled with her glass of orange juice. "Maybe the weather?"

"Maybe farts?" Tamara somehow managed to keep a

straight face.

Blake scrunched her nose. "Do you think vampires fart?"

Shaye giggled. "Are we seriously having a conversation about this?"

"No, I mean it." Blake looked genuinely perplexed. "Do they have normal bodily functions? Do they pee?"

Tamara shook with silent laughter. "Why don't you ask the queen?"

Blake regarded her juice. "I might."

Tamara snorted and turned back to me. "I assume His Highness will be visiting Settlement Four first?"

"No, he won't." I played with my fork. "You get the first home visit. The prince told me this morning."

"What?" Tamara leaned forward, her bosom heaving beneath her purple gown. "When? Tell me everything. *Now.*"

I sighed. "You're leaving later this afternoon. That's all I know."

She pumped her fist. "Yes! Oh, I can't wait for the prince to meet Mother and Father. He'll adore them! They've been very active in supporting the royal family, unlike your peasant, mongrel families..." She chattered away, intermittently insulting us and describing in too-vivid detail all the lingerie she planned to pack.

Instead of smacking her, I counted backward from ten. Because really, when it came to Tamara, what else could I do?

I KEPT TO MYSELF FOR THE REST OF THE AFTERNOON, not wanting to hear Tamara talk about her beautiful home, her amazing parents, and how much the prince was going to adore Settlement 11.

Jealous cow that I was, I couldn't bear to think of the two of them together. The car ride to 11 took hours, and they were spending the night at the Layne mansion. What on earth was Tamara going to get up to with all that free time and proximity to the prince?

It made me sick to even think about, so I paced my chambers instead. I saw the king and the Black Guard when they returned late that afternoon, sentinels meeting them to take the horses back to the stables. I wondered if they'd found any rebels. I shivered, realizing it was really better not to know.

Father, are you out there? Are you still alive?

I also wondered—if he was alive, would he hate me now, as Balkyn seemed to? Would he consider me a traitor to my race? I refused to believe my gentle, brilliant father would be so narrow-minded. But both he and Balkyn had left five years ago to drive the royals off, never to return. Balkyn's hate toward the vampires was vicious and deep. Did my father feel the same way?

I heard a knock at the door, interrupting the unpleasant thoughts. Evangeline hustled in, bearing a letter on a tray. "For you, miss." She smiled kindly. "The prince wanted to make sure you had it as soon as he'd left."

"Thank you." I clutched the letter to my chest and eagerly tore it open once she'd left the room.

My Dearest Gwyneth,

Thank you for a lovely walk this morning. Mother approves of you. Even more importantly, I believe she likes you.

I'm sure the subjects she brought up were a bit nerve-wracking. If you want to talk further about anything we discussed, I am all ears. (And no, I do not mean the bloody werewolves.) But I don't want to pressure you. We'll do it when the time's right.

About my visit to Settlement 11. I'm sure it's unpleasant for you. Were the tables turned, I imagine I would be miserably pacing a hole in the floor—or much worse. But I will be thinking of you while I'm gone. I want you to know that, even if it isn't fair to the other girls for me to say so.

Sometimes fair is overrated.

Stay safe while I'm gone. I look forward to my return so that I may see you again. I will make arrangements for the visit we discussed as soon as I'm back at the castle.

Sincerely,

Your Dallas

I hugged the note against me. No matter what my brother and father felt, this was my happiness. The *prince* was my happiness.

And I believed to my core that he was worthy of my heart. My loyalty. My trust.

I tucked the letter under my pillow, then headed down to dinner, feeling much, much better.

CHAPTER 4
THE ROYAL STALLION

THE NEXT MORNING, SHAYE, BLAKE, AND I ENJOYED French toast with fresh berries, whipped cream—and a side of no Tamara. "It's so soothing without her here. Ah, the sounds of silence. I feel like I'm at a spa." Blake chuckled and helped herself to thirds.

"It's kind of too quiet, though. Tamara can be a bit much, but she does keep us on our toes." Shaye fiddled with her teacup. "What do you think she and the prince are doing?"

"Having breakfast in Tamara's mansion, being waited on hand and foot by adoring servants, while her parents list all of their daughter's undeniable assets to the prince? And perhaps Tamara is strutting about in her workout gear?" I guessed, grimacing. "Not that I'm sour or anything."

Blake pulled a face. "No, of course not."

One of the kitchen maids bustled over and curtsied.

"My ladies. You're wanted in the formal salon in the east wing."

Blake hastily cleaned her plate while Shaye and I watched her shovel her food. She looked up and found us staring. "What?"

"You eat like every meal's your last." Shaye giggled.

"It *is* my last week at the palace. I have to stock up."

Shaye arched an eyebrow. "His Highness might choose you, you know. You do have that hot supermodel thing going on."

"The prince has kissed all of you—the closest he's come to me is slapping me a high five." Blake snorted. "I am not a love match for him. I think he's kept me around to make sure the three of you don't scratch each other's eyes out."

We giggled and chatted as we headed to the formal east salon. But inside, my heart ached. I had only one week left with my friends, whom I'd grown to genuinely love. I couldn't bear to think of us all separated. One of us would be staying at the palace, but only one. I swallowed hard as we made it to the room.

Tariq waited inside, rubbing his hands together. "Good morning, ladies."

We curtsied and took our seats.

"I want to thank each of you for the excellent job you've done so far as finalists. We've gotten lots of great footage for the next episode. We will be broadcasting every night this week so that the audience is watching in almost real time. We want to heighten the excitement, the drama, leading up to the finale."

The royal emissary paced in front of us, looking slightly overcaffeinated and positively gleeful. "First things first, let's discuss how the rest of the week will proceed. It's going to go fast. We have the home visits, and as you know, each of you will have a meeting with the queen. You will each also have a final date with the prince before the finale, when he chooses his future wife. We'll arrange these events around the royals' schedule. It's going to be hectic. Do your best to get plenty of rest and be prepared to be summoned at a moment's notice."

Tariq grabbed a remote and turned on the large flat screen. "The prince and Tamara will be returning from their trip to Settlement Eleven this evening. I want to share footage with you from the visit thus far."

Shaye, Blake, and I exchanged a quick glance. "We've got film back already?" I asked. "They only left last night."

"I know, but Mira's just sent the footage. Remember, this is the rough cut. It hasn't been edited yet. But the production crew is going to get to work straightaway so that the episode can go live. Now I want you to pay attention, because Tamara nailed this performance. Your home visits are coming up quickly—in fact, one of you will be leaving with the prince first thing tomorrow morning."

Shaye raised her hand. "Can you tell us who?"

"I'm finalizing things with the production team in a bit. You'll know as soon as I do." He hit a button on the remote. "Really, you should be taking notes. Once you see this, you'll understand what I mean. It's a game changer."

My stomach dropped as the film rolled, showing the front of the palace. Dallas and Tamara stood on the stairs, their hands firmly entwined. Dallas looked tall, dark, and devastatingly handsome in his steel-gray cere-monial uniform. He stared straight ahead, his jaw tight. Tamara wore a dark-blue dress and traveling coat, her hair in an elegant chignon, her sapphire earrings catching the light. She looked graceful and sophisticated, genuine princess material.

Mira Kinney stood next to them, smiling widely for the camera, her white teeth flashing in contrast to her high-collared black coat. "Good evening, and welcome back to the Pageant! We're here with His Royal Highness Prince Black and Miss Tamara Layne. We're heading into the final stretch of the competition: the home visits. The prince and Miss Layne are traveling to Settlement Eleven to meet with Miss Layne's family."

Mira turned to Tamara. "Miss Layne, how are you feeling about going home?"

Tamara beamed as she leaned toward the micro-phone. "I'm thrilled, Mira, really. I've missed my family so much. I'm so excited for them to meet Dallas."

I grimaced at her use of his first name. "I just know they're going to love him as much as I do," she gushed.

Mira's eyeballs almost popped out her head, but she recovered quickly. "Your Highness, what are you most looking forward to?"

Dallas smiled for the camera. "It will be an honor to

meet Miss Layne's family and to hear about their chari-
table work in Settlement Eleven. I'm anxious to visit
Eleven itself and to learn more about the people who
live there."

I took cold comfort in the fact that he'd called her
"Miss Layne" and that he hadn't listed snogging her face
off as one of the things he was excited about.

"Excellent." Mira turned back to the camera. "I have
a special treat for the viewers at home. The prince has
allowed us to film the happy couple during their car ride,
so you'll be able to take the journey *with* them, literally.
It's so very generous of His Highness and so exciting for
us! Stay tuned for all the private moments between His
Highness and Miss Layne."

As this was an unedited version, the next scene
abruptly cut to the backseat of the car whisking the
prince and Tamara to Settlement 11. Tamara scooted next
to Dallas, smoothing his jacket. "There, that's better."
Beaming up at him, she was the cat who had cornered
the canary. "We can't have you looking rumpled for
Mother and Father."

"Thank you." Dallas sat back and turned toward her,
putting a small amount of space between them—much to
my relief. "Why don't you tell me more about them?"

A genuine smile lit up her beautiful face, making her
look like the angel she was not. "They're just lovely. My
mother was the president of a large bank before the war,
and my father owned his own company. Brilliant, both
of them."

"It sounds as if you have much to be proud of."

Dallas's eyes darkened. "But what have they done since then?"

"You don't have to be worried. Both my mother and father are at peace with the sacrifices they've made," Tamara assured him. "My family fully supports yours. We knew it was time for a change. The settlements were struggling, people were suffering. You have the Layne family's loyalty, Your Highness. We are very vocal about it."

His face softened a fraction. "Thank you. That means a lot. Now, please tell me more about your life at home."

She cleared her throat and continued. "When the war came and continuing in their former professions was no longer an option, my parents threw themselves fully into charity work. They've privately funded a school in Eleven and have established multiple scholarships. Before I joined the competition, I tutored needy children every day after my own lessons." She lifted her chin proudly. "I daresay I have a bit of a cult following in my settlement. I hold the record for most students who've passed their exams."

Dallas's smile was genuine this time. "That's quite admirable."

Tamara looked pleased. "Thank you, Your Highness. I enjoy the children. They make me fan art. It's quite adorable, really."

Blake made a gagging gesture, but it didn't make me feel any better. Tamara was killing it. Who didn't love someone who helped needy children?

Tamara frowned at Dallas coyly. "You seem surprised, Your Highness."

The prince's face darkened. "Forgive me. I'm afraid I underestimated you."

"It happens all the time." Tamara shrugged prettily. "People judge me based on how I look. They think because I'm wealthy and successful that I don't understand hardship. Or that I don't want to help. It's quite the opposite. My life's mission is to carry on my parents' vision and expand upon that. I would love to see each settlement in the land working together to help our youth. The children are our future, really. It's a simple fact—we can't move forward without them being positioned for success. I for one want to do everything in my power to see the coming generations of the settlements prosper."

"She's quite good at this," Blake muttered.

Dallas seemed to agree. He regarded Tamara seriously, as if seeing her for the first time. "I would love to work with you on this issue. I think it's a fantastic idea."

Tamara preened at his compliment, her eyes sparkling. "Thank you, Your Highness. That would be an honor. Now." She scooted closer, closing the distance between them. She smoothed his jacket again, keeping her hands firmly planted on his broad chest. "How else can we get to know each other on this trip?" She gazed up at him with a mixture of adoration and thinly veiled lust.

The prince cleared his throat. He looked like a rabbit

about to get caught in a snare. "You could tell me about your hobbies?"

"Ah." She arched an eyebrow. "I did have a favorite pastime as a young girl."

He watched her warily. "Yes? What was it?"

"I always dreamed about growing up and becoming a princess. Perhaps dreams do come true." She slid onto his lap and straddled him, her beautiful face inches from his. They stared at each other, and I watched his expression change from wary to strained. I could almost feel the heat between them.

Sharp pain pierced my heart. I wanted to turn away, to close my eyes, but I couldn't.

It's a show. A game. It's political. I clenched my hands into fists as the moment between them stretched out inexorably, intolerably.

Finally, Dallas recovered. He chuckled as he gently moved her off. "Miss Layne. I thought you didn't want me rumpled?"

Undeterred, she put a finger under his chin, drawing his face close. "I can fix you afterward. I quite enjoy having my hands on you, Your Highness."

"I have to be a gentleman." He captured her hand under his. "I value your honor, my lady."

"Then trust me, I won't do anything I don't want to do." She pulled him in for a deep, passionate kiss. Dallas put his hands on her back just as the screen went black.

I struggled to catch my breath. I'd seen Dallas kiss both Tamara and Shaye in the other episodes, but this *hurt*. I didn't want him in a bloody car with Tamara all the way to Settlement 11. I didn't want him in her bloody house. I felt as if someone was using my heart like a voodoo doll, a pincushion for rusty, sharp little needles.

Tariq bounded to the front of the room, his eyes glittering in triumph. "See? I told you—A-Game, ladies. She was *flawless*."

Blake snorted. "She was something, all right."

"Now, now." Tariq clucked his tongue. "Don't let your emotions get in the way of your judgment. Mira said so herself when she sent the tape—Tamara is hitting the right notes. She's showing herself as a potential leader. The viewers are getting to know the things that are important to her and would be important to her as a princess. And you don't doubt that she has sincere feelings for the prince. That's the standard, girls." He pointed at the screen. "If you can't do better than that, you can kiss His Highness goodbye."

His gaze found mine. "No matter what you might've believed, understand this. The prince will choose the winner based on what he believes is best for the settlements. If that's not you, you'd best prepare to pack your bags. Now if you'll excuse me, I have to meet with the production crew. You're off to your lesson with Ms. Blakely. I'll check in with you later."

I watched his back as he hustled from the room, a bitter taste in my mouth.

"Well, that was...illuminating." Shaye looked thoughtful as she gathered her things to head to our lesson. "Who knew Tamara was such an amazing politician?"

I frowned. "I suppose the prince wasn't the only one who's underestimated her."

Shaye frowned back. "So what do we do?"

Blake sighed. "I think the only thing we can do is be ourselves. The prince is going to choose one of us. Now, I don't believe for a moment that it's going to be me, and I can live with that. I like His Highness, but I'm not emotionally attached to him. So just be yourself. If he likes you best, he'll choose you. It's pretty simple when you think of it that way."

I nodded, slowly following them to the hall as we headed for our lesson. But as much as I wanted to believe Blake—to believe that the prince's choice was simple— part of me feared it would be based on factors more complicated than his feelings. And I worried that I was going to end up on the wrong side of that.

The packing-your-bags side.

"Are you all right?" Shaye asked quietly.

"Yes, of course." But even my easy answer had me wondering.

Was I lying to Shaye? Or was I lying to myself?

CHAPTER 5
COLD AS ICE

I BARELY TOUCHED MY DINNER, A FACT THAT DID NOT go unnoticed by my friends. But I escaped their worried glances, returning to my room early, all the better to pace and fret alone.

I read and reread Dallas's letter. *I will be thinking of you while I'm gone. I want you to know that, even if it isn't fair to the other girls.* Was he thinking of me as Tamara straddled him or when she was espousing the benefits of helping underprivileged children?

Or was he thinking that she was hot and that she'd make a fantastic princess?

I tried to calm my rioting thoughts. This was not the first time my jealousy had gotten the better of me during the competition. I *was* human, after all. But this felt different. We had so little time left, and the end was coming for me, whether I was ready or not.

I understood that choosing a bride was complicated for someone in Dallas's position. I also understood that I might not be the best choice for a princess. Although I could grasp the logic of that, I couldn't bear to face the truth behind it.

I couldn't bear to think of leaving him.

After wandering around my room for hours, I finally made myself get into bed. But not long after I'd fallen into a restless sleep, I heard a knock on my door.

"Miss, I'm so sorry to wake you in the middle of the night, but the sentinels are here. They said they're waiting to bring you somewhere, and you must get up and get dressed." Evangeline bustled in and peered at me, her pretty face creased with worry. "Is everything quite all right?"

"Yes, of course." My heart raced with anticipation. "Is the prince back?"

She nodded. "I had word that they returned late last night."

I looked out the window, but it was still black outside. "What time is it?"

"Four a.m., miss."

"I'm so sorry that they woke you. Please tell them I'll be right out—I'll be quick." I grabbed a dress and headed for the bathroom. I threw the dress on, brushed my teeth, and splashed some cold water on my face, my nerves thrumming. *Balkyn. The prince must have arranged for me to see my brother.*

When I came out, Evangeline had the fire roaring, and she'd neatly made my bed. "Evangeline, thank you. But go back to bed. You don't need to start your day now. It's still night."

Her face pinched with obvious concern. "Are you sure everything's all right?"

"Of course it is. I'll see you at tea. Thank you for everything."

She curtsied, and although I knew she was curious as well as worried about me, I didn't say anything further. No one but the royal family, the Black Guard, and some of the royal advisors knew what had happened with the rebels. I hadn't told my maids or any of my human friends about Balkyn. I didn't want to put their safety in jeopardy or have the royals find out that others in the palace were privy to information that had been kept from them.

After Evangeline left, I took a deep breath, hesitating. I desperately wanted to see Balkyn, and yet... We'd parted on such bad terms. I recalled some of his last words to me. *"You have sold your soul to the devil... I only know you are no sister of mine."*

I had to make him see that I was still the younger sibling he loved. I was still Gwyneth, his little sister, and I could help him. I nodded to the guards who waited outside.

"This way, my lady."

I followed the three men through the hall, then down the grand staircase. The palace was eerily dark and quiet at this hour. It seemed as if even the vampires had gone to bed. We made our way toward the dungeon. I held my breath, as if breathing would be too loud and out of place in the silence of the stone hallway. I prayed we didn't run into anyone. What on earth would the king say if he found me with a royal escort, parading around the palace in the middle of the night?

I briefly wondered where Dallas was, but he was likely in a meeting with the king. Hopefully he'd keep the king busy so that I wouldn't get caught wandering after curfew.

Finally, we reached the stairwell to the dungeon. I shivered as I remembered the last time I'd been down these stairs—it had been to see the prisoner Benjamin Vale. He'd escaped and killed three guards, then Dallas had executed him at the request of the king. I forced the thoughts away. I had to stay focused on my brother and on finding some common ground with him.

A tall, shadowy figure waited on the stair landing, and my heart leapt in my throat. Was it a friend or foe? But then he stepped into the torchlight, and I recognized his handsome face. I sighed in relief. "Hello, Dallas."

He frowned. "Gwyneth. A word, please, before you go downstairs."

He nodded to the soldiers, and they retreated, guarding the entrance to the stairwell. He reached for my hands, but I stepped back, putting some distance between us.

He cursed. "I guess you've seen the tape."

"We saw some of it." I cleared my throat. "It was nothing I haven't seen before."

"And yet you won't come near me." Dallas took a step closer, and my heart rate kicked up. He put his hand on my waist, and my knees buckled. I longed to press my face against his chest, to have him stroke my hair and tell me that everything was going to be okay—with my brother, with the competition, with *him*.

But as he wasn't my fairy godmother, it didn't seem appropriate to be such a whiner. "It's not you. I'm worried...I'm worried about Balkyn." Emotions vied for predominance inside me, but I could concentrate on only one at a time. "Can we please go see him before the whole castle wakes up and I get you into even more trouble with your father?"

The torchlight cast shadows across Dallas's face. He didn't look pleased. "Fine. Follow me."

I hesitated. "I don't think it's a good idea for Balkyn to see us together."

His face darkened further. "Of course. I'll stay out of sight."

I took a deep breath. I didn't want to hurt his feelings, but my brother had not reacted well to my attachment to the prince. "I think his position is intolerable, but I'm not here for that. I'm here because he's not eating, and I'm worried about him. Can you understand?"

Dallas nodded. "Yes, I understand. If I may say so, I don't think it's a good idea for you to see him, but..."

"But?"

"It is your choice, and I respect that. Come." He motioned for the guards, and we headed down the stairs.

Dallas glanced over his shoulder at me as we descended, that same grim expression on his face. "You must be prepared—he doesn't look well. He's lost quite a bit of weight." I held my breath again, not knowing what would be waiting for me in the dungeon.

At the bottom of the stairs, Dallas bowed and stepped to the side. "I'll be waiting here. If you need me, do not hesitate."

"Th-thank you." My whole body jittered with adrenaline as we entered the prison block. It was as I remembered, with stone floors and walls and the stench of stale body odor. The guards approached the third cell and nodded to me.

"Prisoner," one of them called. "You have a visitor."

"Like I bloody care." *Balkyn.* He sounded surly, but he also sounded weak.

I rushed to his cell. "Balkyn? It's me."

My brother huddled under a thin blanket. When he sat up on his bunk, I gasped. He had wasted away. His eyes were huge, the skin around them drawn tightly. His cheeks were protruding, and the rest of his face was shallow and sunken, a far cry from the rugged soldier I'd last seen a few weeks ago. "Oh my God! You look terrible."

He let the blanket fall to his waist, and I could see his scrawny chest, his ribs protruding sharply beneath his thin T-shirt. "What?" His voice was scratchy. "Do normal humans disgust you now, sister?"

"Of course not. But forgive me, it is hard for me to see you like this." I fought back tears. I was angry, shocked, and saddened, everything jumbling together. I shut my eyes, then took a deep breath and faced him again. "Tell me what I can do to help."

"You can tell your bloodsucker boyfriend to give us our country back, for starters."

I gripped the bars to his cell. "Balkyn. I cannot undo a revolution. But I *can* help you."

"I don't want your bloody help." His voice sounded choked.

I reached through the bars toward him. "Brother, please."

"I wish I'd never seen you again." To my horror, tears ran down his face. He savagely wiped them away, as if they disgusted him.

"I am still your family. We have the same blood, the same home. I still love you. Let me help you. I can get you something better to eat. The food here's delicious—"

He sprang up and lunged toward the bars. "You don't get it, Gwyneth! I am in hell! I'd no sooner eat the vampire's food than I would sit and dine with the devil. They've bewitched you. It's some sort of dark magic so that you cannot see the truth of what surrounds you!"

I took a step back from him, from his fury. "I told you. The prince and his family have been nothing but kind. I see it quite clearly."

He leaned forward, into the light, his face strained and shadows visibly etched beneath his eyes. "You have been blinded by their power and their magic."

"*You're* the one who cannot see. You won't accept anything that contravenes your hate."

"I gave up my life to fight them. I gave my life to protect my family. And now you have turned on me and turned on your own kind. And for what." He looked me up and down, pure disgust on his face. "For a fancy dress and a hot meal? For a handsome prince? You disgust me, Gwyneth. You are a vampire's whore."

"That's enough." Dallas stormed into the room, his cape flying behind him. "Unlock the door."

The nearest sentinel obeyed swiftly.

I clutched at him. "Dallas, no—"

He ignored me, sweeping into the cell. Balkyn faced him, no trace of fear in his eyes, only hate.

"No. Please." I ran and shoved Dallas, but I might as well have been shoving a brick wall.

Balkyn sneered at me even as Dallas cornered him. "Don't you defend me. I want nothing from you—not your help, not your pity, certainly not your whorish clout with the prince."

"Balkyn, no." Tears coursed down my face. The hatred in his voice physically stung. *My own flesh and blood.* "Not like this."

Balkyn shook his head, his gaze flicking over the prince. "What did you think was going to come of mixing with their kind?"

"Mr. West." Dallas took a step forward. My brother was tall, but the prince made him look tiny, frail. "You seem to have forgotten yourself."

"Don't you speak to me, devil. You've ruined my sister!"

Dallas grabbed my brother by the throat and shoved him against the wall. "You hate me and my kind, and you very well might have your reasons."

Balkyn struggled in Dallas's grasp. "I do hate your kind, you filthy bloodsucker," he wheezed. "I'd spit on you if your devil-made hands weren't so tight around my throat."

"Dallas, please—"

The prince turned to me, and I could see it in his face: he was using every ounce of self-control he had not to snap my brother's neck.

"Please don't kill him."

His eyes blazed, but he nodded, once, almost imperceptibly.

"Don't spare me on account of that whore." Balkyn's words were strangled. "I'd rather be dead than see my own sister like this."

Dallas turned back, and they faced one another, each white with rage.

"You forget yourself, and you also forget your sister. She is *innocent*. She is *good*, all that remains so in the world. You will not speak to her like that in my home, or anywhere else, ever again." Dallas squeezed tighter. "Now, apologize."

Balkyn could barely catch his breath, but he still managed to say, "Sod off, bloodsucker."

Dallas opened his mouth and hissed so his fangs blazed. "Apologize to your sister. And do it now, or I'm going to drink just enough of your blood to turn you into one of my kind."

Balkyn still looked at him with fierce, intractable hatred, but a glimmer of fear lurked beneath. His eyes bulged as Dallas gripped harder.

"Gwyneth," Balkyn choked out. "I'm sorry."

Dallas released him, and he dropped to the ground.

"B-Balkyn." I reached for my brother, but he shrank back, as if he were afraid I was contagious. "P-please."

Dallas gently clasped my hands. "Gwyneth, we should go."

I nodded, my shoulders shaking with sobs. The prince carefully led me from the cell and Balkyn's hate-filled glare.

I wiped my face roughly. There were so many things I wanted to say to my brother, but I didn't dare.

"Go away and don't ever come back," he croaked from the floor as the sentinels locked his cell door.

I looked up at Dallas. "Wait."

He nodded, the muscle in his jaw so tight it appeared close to snapping.

I took a deep breath, straightened myself, and turned toward the cell. "Brother. We might not believe the same things, and you might very well hate me. That is your choice. But you are my family, and I will never truly abandon you. That is *my* choice. I love you, brother. Even as you curse me, I love you."

Balkyn watched me as I reached for Dallas's hand and gripped it. But somehow, I managed not to cry again until we'd turned the corner and I was safely away from the brother who'd broken my heart.

CHAPTER 6
DARK SHADOWS

DALLAS DISMISSED THE GUARDS AND PULLED ME INTO one of the studies. He closed the door and came toward me cautiously, as if unsure of what I wanted.

But only one thing could possibly make me feel any better. I reached for him.

He exhaled deeply as I buried my face against his chest. He let me cry, not saying a word as I let it all out. Not only was I heartbroken, but I was also enraged. My brother was a bigot. Blinded by his prejudice, he couldn't even imagine that what I'd told him was the truth.

Not hating vampires was beyond his comprehension.

Eventually, I stopped crying. Dallas gave me a handkerchief and some space. He went to the window as I blew my nose, willing myself to let go of the meeting with my brother. "Thank you for letting me see him and for standing up for me."

"I wasn't sure you'd be thanking me." Dallas gazed out the window, watching the sun come up. "But no one is allowed to speak to you like that, not while I dwell on this earth. Not even your own brother."

"He doesn't want to be my brother anymore."

Dallas's gaze flicked over me, probably taking in my ruined, puffy face. "He's not himself, Gwyneth. Starving in a cell will do that to you."

I sank into a nearby chair. "I don't think letting him loose would change his attitude too much." Now that I'd seen Balkyn, the situation seemed even more dire.

"What would you have me do?" Dallas asked.

"I don't know. If we let him go, he'll run right back to the rebels and tell them all sorts of things about the palace, about you..." I stared miserably at the floor. "And I don't think he'd stay with my mother if you let him return home."

Dallas raised his gaze to meet mine. "I don't want you to hate me for keeping him prisoner."

"I could never hate you."

He raked a hand through his hair. "Don't be so sure."

A chill needled my spine. "What does that mean?"

He went back to looking out the window.

"Dallas?"

He sighed. "If your brother starves himself to death in my dungeon, I feel certain that you would grow to hate me."

"Like I said, that's impossible, but let's not go there yet. We can still save him. There must be a way."

"We have another problem."

My heart beat erratically in my chest. "What?"

"I had a meeting with my father when I returned

from Eleven." The muscle in his jaw jumped. "He expressed that he would like me to choose Tamara at the end of the competition."

The floor spun beneath me, and I was grateful for the chair. "I see."

"I'm only telling you this because I need you to understand what we're up against." Dallas shook his head. "I have no intention of listening to him. But his position makes things...more difficult."

My head throbbed. "Why Tamara? Why not Blake or Shaye?" The king did not care for me for several legitimate reasons. I'd helped Benjamin Vale escape from his cell, causing the death of three palace guards. I'd been captured by the rebels, and Dallas had been injured when he rescued me. So I understood why the king wouldn't choose me for his son, but the other two girls were both wonderful. Although it was painful to think about, I believed either one of them would be a better choice for Dallas than Tamara.

He raked a hand through his hair. "After learning more about her parents, he feels that Tamara's family connections would be the most advantageous for our political position. It has nothing to do with her personally—he probably doesn't even know which girl she is. All he cares about is the war."

Sensing his misery, I stood and went to him. "He cares about you, too."

Dallas wrapped his arms around me. "You don't know him, but I appreciate the comfort, all the same."

I put my head against his broad chest. "So will you...

consider it? Your family's position needs to be strengthened. Tamara *would* be an advantageous match." My tongue felt funny, as if it were too big for my mouth, as I forced the words out.

"*No.*"

The fierceness of his tone made me shiver. I did not want to be parted from Dallas, but if Tamara was the right choice for him, as well as the settlements, how could I stand in the way? "I wish we didn't have to have this conversation, but you should think about your father's wishes, and your other...your other options." I swallowed hard.

"Shh." He breathed against my hair. "Do not say another word, and do not leave my embrace."

I smiled, even as I felt my heart breaking. "Yes, Your Dallas."

He kissed the top of my head. "That's my good girl."

I clung to him, never wanting to let go. Although I longed to lose myself in his arms, emotion churned through me. Too much weighed on my shoulders. My own brother hated me. The king wanted the prince to marry Tamara. Everyone was against us, and yet here we were, wrapped in each other's embrace. There was nowhere I'd rather have been, but so much threatened to wrench us apart.

Deep down, I worried that letting myself love the prince was dangerous. To love him this much, with the very real possibility of losing him, was akin to emotional suicide. These weren't the sort of wounds that I could recover from, ever.

I released him and took a step back. "I should go."

Dallas's gaze darkened. "Gwyneth."

My eyes filled with tears. "Do you think that I want to leave you? Do you think that I want to be a runner-up, to watch you with the other girls? To watch Tamara straddle you? To watch you choose someone else as your wife?"

He reached for my hands and gripped them. "No, I don't."

"I have to do what's right for you." My voice shook. "And how can that mean asking you to choose me when my brother's starving himself down in your dungeon, and he'd rather stake you than accept your gruel?"

"You are right for me because *I say so*." He glowered. "No one—not the king, not your brother, not bloody Tariq—can tell me otherwise."

I straightened my spine and banished my tears. "But I can."

Dallas sighed, sounding exasperated. "Are you trying to give me a headache?"

"No, I am trying to save your life."

He scoffed. "Explain yourself. Quickly, so I have a chance to kiss you multiple times before I have to go to another bloody meeting."

I winced—I wanted nothing more than to hurl myself into his arms and snog him until neither of us could see straight—but too much was at risk. "Your father wants you to choose Tamara for a reason. Politically, she's an advantageous match."

"She's a pushy, spoiled—"

I held my hand up to stop him. "She can help you. Her *family* can help you. I remember when we first met. You told me that's what this competition was all about, bringing peace and harmony to the settlements. The Pageant is political, Dallas. Feelings are important, but they're not the most important thing. You started this for a reason—to protect the settlements and secure your family's position. You told me that yourself."

Dallas straightened to his formidable height. "To marry a settler—a human—would be, in and of itself, a huge political accomplishment. *Any human settler.* That's why I brought you all here. So that I could choose which one of you made me happy, the one that I could spend the rest of my life with. I was not shopping for a political running mate. I was looking for my *wife*. My father understood and approved of my motivations, but now that he's seen he can gain an edge, he's pushing for more. Which is so very typical of him, it's sickening."

"Then for argument's sake, let's forget about what Tamara can do for you. Let's forget about any 'edge' that any of the finalists can give you. But consider this. All things being equal, I am still a poor choice. My brother is a confirmed rebel. He's a prisoner here. My father is a rebel, and he's still at large. My family is a liability, Dallas. I don't want that to be true. I don't want this to be impossible. I never would have come here if I'd known, if I'd even thought..."

He stood over me. "If you'd thought what?"

"That I would feel this way about you. That things would have gotten to this point."

He tucked a hair behind my ear. "Please don't ever say that again."

"Which thing?"

"That you would never have come here. Because then I never would have met you, and that's something I can't bear to think about." He tapped me under the chin, raising my gaze to meet his. "I don't care about any of it—your family, my family, the rebels, the crown."

"But you have to."

"I don't have to do anything other than exactly what I bloody well want. We can leave, Gwyneth. We can leave all of this behind and go find some happy little bubble where no one will care who we are or what we do. I would go with you now, if you say the word."

My heart twisted. "But we can't."

"We're adults—yes we can."

I shook my head. "I'm barely an adult, and my mother and younger siblings need me. I can't leave them behind. And you can't run away from your obligations. The settlements need you."

The more I'd gotten to know Dallas—his goodness, strength, and kindness—the more I believed this to be true. He would be the one to save the settlements, to restore them to their former peace and prosperity. He'd been kept in the dark about our nation's condition, but through the course of the competition, he'd learned more about the true state of affairs of most of our people. He wanted to make changes, to help people, to make the settlements better.

"I would love nothing more than to find a happy

bubble for us to call our own, but I'm afraid my conscience wouldn't allow it," I said. "I can't be so selfish. You're too good. I can't keep you all to myself—the world needs you."

He kissed my forehead. "And I need you." My eyes filled with tears, and he grimaced. "Here we go again."

"Please hear me out." I gripped his hands. "I cannot have it on my conscience to undo you. When it comes out that my father and brother are rebels—and eventually, it *will* come out—it will divide the settlements. People will wonder whether they can trust me or if you have a traitor in your own court, in your own bed. What kind of princess would that make me? How unsteady would your position be then?"

I hadn't thought about all of this before, but now the enormity of the problem became only too clear. "Not to mention the fact that your parents will never accept me. Would they even accept a child, if we were to have one?" I released him and started pacing, muttering to myself while issues I hadn't even foreseen came crashing down around me.

Dallas watched me, frowning, until I noticed and stopped pacing. "What is it?"

"Come here."

I went to him, my brow still furrowed. He pulled me close, running his hands over my face, smoothing it, trying to soothe me. "You can pace and fret and mutter all you want. But we *will* be successful, and this *will* be okay."

"How can you say that? How do you know?"

He leaned over me, brushing his lips against mine. "Because I know. And because I am the prince, and I say so. Now kiss me, Gwyneth. If we have nothing else—if everything is as dire as you predict—we at least have this moment together. I will not waste it."

He crushed his lips against mine, and I reached up, sinking my hands into his thick hair. He deepened the kiss, and I moaned. Every kiss, every touch, every second I let myself love him, I put us both at risk.

I knew this. And I knew very, very well that I might not be able to have him. That I might walk away with nothing, and it could happen soon.

But I still arched my back, getting as close as I possibly could, and kissed him as if my life depended on it. Caution, or perhaps myself, be damned.

CHAPTER 7
REALIZATIONS

HEARING A KNOCK ON THE DOOR, WE JUMPED APART. Tariq stuck his head into the room, and Dallas muttered some colorful curse words I'd never heard before. He clenched his fists and glared at the royal emissary. "What?"

Tariq bowed, and when he straightened, he managed to look apologetic. "Your Highness. Miss West. You two are up early."

"Yes, Tariq, we are. And we were quite involved with *important business* before you bloody came in here!"

"My apologies, but I have time-sensitive news." The royal emissary absently rubbed his ear, perhaps remembering how Dallas had pinched it some weeks ago.

Dallas looked close to grabbing it again. "Go on."

"I've just gotten word that your next home visit will be to Settlement Four."

Oh dear. That meant all sorts of time for us alone together. I didn't know whether to laugh or cry.

"Ah. Thank you, Tariq." Dallas suddenly looked infinitely less pissed.

Tariq nodded. "Your Highness, the king would like to see you for another meeting with the advisory board before you depart. Miss West, you should assemble your maids and start packing."

I curtsied. "Yes, Your Royal Emissary. Thank you." But I didn't want to thank him. I *wanted* to get my head on straight and put some distance between the prince and myself.

He might be forced to choose someone else. And maybe it's for the best.

But being so close to him, kissing him, having him protect me from my brother and showing him mercy— every part of me longed to go to Dallas, to beg him to choose me, to let me stay with him forever. The alternative was unbearable. And yet so very many obstacles stood in our way.

The depth of my feelings for him overwhelmed me, as if I were swimming out into the middle of the ocean; I was in dangerously over my head. I needed to calm myself and get grounded lest I be swallowed by the undertow and pulled out to sea forever, losing myself and destroying Dallas's chance to become a great leader in the process.

But instead of being able to catch my breath, I was going home with him. Dallas's gaze flicked to me, a small smile on his lips. *He* didn't look sorry about it in the least. "I'll see you shortly, Gwyneth."

I curtsied again. "Yes, Your Highness." Did I imagine it, or did he look awfully excited?

I cleared my throat and turned back to Tariq. "Will we be staying with my family?"

Tariq shook his head. "No, I'm afraid not. The production team decided that since you've been there before, a change of scenery would be better for ratings. But you *will* dine with your family this evening."

"Thank you. I'm looking forward to seeing them. But...where will we be staying in Four?" I felt my cheeks heat as I tried and failed to keep my mind from imagining all manner of possibilities.

Tariq smiled at me with feigned patience. "We will brief you before you leave, Miss West. Your maids have been given instructions about what to pack."

I nodded at him. Tariq motioned to the prince, asking him about something administrative, and I used it as my chance to escape. I hustled down the hall, then thinking better of it, turned and went toward Eve's chambers. I hadn't seen her in a few days, and we needed to talk. Eve always had a way of putting things into perspective.

The sentinels at the entrance to her chamber nodded and opened the doors. I found my friend in the middle of her room, upside down in a headstand.

"What on earth are you doing?" I cried.

"Balance training." She was perfectly still, every muscle actively holding her in place. "It'll make me a better fighter."

I flopped into a nearby chair. "Again, I don't know

why you're working so hard. You're bloody strong as it is."

Eve sighed, slowly lowering her legs to the ground. She pulled herself right side up, her blond curls bouncing. "Any fool can be strong. I want to be *good*."

"You are good. You're magnificent, Eve."

She plopped down in the chair across from me, grinning. "Tell me what's wrong. I know you're not here to gush about my magnificence."

"I have to get to my room and pack, but I wanted to see you first." I leaned back in the chair. "Dallas took me to see my brother this morning. It did not go well."

Eve's face softened, even as her unusual aqua eyes burned with intensity. "I heard he's having a hard time. What happened?"

"More of the same. He hates me, he hates Dallas, he hates vampires. He's stopped eating. He's lost so much weight he's barely more than a skeleton, but he won't let me help him. He told me he never wants to see me again."

"He doesn't mean it," Eve said. "He's blinded by his own hate. It's distorted his reasoning."

"His hate is very sincere. I don't detect anything in him that shows me he could ever change his mind."

Eve blew out a deep breath. "With time, that could change. Once he sees what we're really like."

"I don't know. He said that vampires are the devil, and he meant it."

"Maybe I could try to talk to him. You know, a disinterested third party?" She sounded hopeful.

"That's very kind of you, but I don't think he'd be anything but horrible. You don't deserve that."

Eve shrugged. "I'm not afraid of him. Remember how I used to speak of vampires? Maybe I can find some common ground with him. Think about it?"

"Thank you." I smiled. "You always make me feel better."

"So tell me what else is bothering you and whether it has anything to do with the fact that you look like you've recently been snogged within an inch of your life."

I sighed. "I was just with Dallas."

"Well, I would hope so." Eve chuckled.

"I think I have to break it off with him."

She groaned. "He'll lock you in the dungeons next to Balkyn if you try to leave."

"I'm not trying to leave. But speaking of snogging, he went home with Tamara yesterday, and they got way too close for comfort."

"We've talked about this, Gwyn. You know he has to sample the merchandise, as they say. They've got to keep the audience guessing—unlike the rest of us, who know he only has eyes for you. It makes the contest a bit boring, actually, having him moon about you all the time." She yawned. "So you're going to have to do better than that."

"Fine." I straightened my spine. "Here's the real reason I'm thinking this way. I'm worried that I'm going to bring harm to him, and that's the last thing I want."

"Tell me more."

"I'm bad for him. My brother hates vampires, my

father is a rebel, and both of them would stake Dallas and his whole family if they had the chance."

"He's not dating your father or your brother. He's in a relationship with you."

I hopped up and started pacing. "But that's the problem, isn't it? If I were to become the princess and the news broke about my family, it would put Dallas in a horrible position. What I'm saying is, I have to protect him. From me."

Eve shook her head. "He's pretty capable of taking care of himself. And he's an adult. You need to respect him to make his own choices."

"But feelings aren't choices." I paced some more.

"Of course they are. Your brain's not the only organ that gets to make decisions, you know."

"Are you suggesting that any organ should be able to choose?" I scoffed. "A pancreas? A kidney? An appendix?"

Eve frowned. "I've no idea what any of those squishy things would want. But your heart wants things. And it's no less important than your brain, if you ask me."

I shook my head. "I don't know about that."

"Sure you do. Why does your heart care for me? Why does it care for the prince? Why does it break for your brother, even when he's insanely cruel to you? Your heart knows things, Gwyn. To ignore it is to ignore the very real gift that you've been given—by God, the fates, your maker. Your heart's what makes you *you*. Who you love is who you are."

"This whole immortality thing really has made you philosophical."

Eve jutted her chin. "I told you so."

I turned on my heel. "If we're so intent on listening to my feelings, I can tell you this. I feel strongly that I need to protect the prince. If I brought him harm, it would undo me."

"More than giving him away to someone else?"

"I have to be a grown-up about this. It's not a game." My heart squeezed. "You've told me from the beginning to remember that the contest is political. You were right. Dallas agreed to participate in the Pageant for a reason—the betterment of the settlements, national unity, moving forward into a new era in which the royals are embraced as the true leaders of our country. If the princess is the daughter of a rebel, how does *that* work? It only high-lights our divide. It doesn't bring our nation together. It tears us further apart."

Eve shook her head, her curls bouncing. "If the prince chooses you, he shows the country that he accepts us as he finds us—and loves us, anyway. I don't see it the way you do. If the prince is brave enough to love a rebel's daughter, it shows how strong he is. How certain he is not only of his commitment to his new bride but also to the history of our nation."

I kept pacing. "The king does not approve of me, Eve. He never will."

"If Dallas doesn't care, why should you?"

"Because I'm the one putting him into that terrible position—at odds with his own family." I wrung my hands. "What if the king decides to turn the crown over to his younger brother instead, as a punishment?"

"It wouldn't be the end of the world. I'm sure the prince himself would tell you that."

"But *I* think it would be the end of the world. Dallas should be the one to rule. You know him. You know how talented and kind he is, how much he truly cares for the people in our country. No one is better suited to unite us."

Eve smiled. "It sounds as if you trust his judgment."

"Of course I do."

"Then let him choose the winner, and have faith that everything will work out in the end."

"Oh, Eve, I wish I could." I sighed. "I have to go."

She winked at me. "Have fun."

But fun wasn't on my mind as I hustled to my chambers; fear was. Fear that the king would tear us apart. Fear that he *wouldn't* and that I was the wrong choice for Dallas.

I made a promise to myself. I would enjoy this trip— I'd soak up every second, basking in my proximity to the prince. But I would remember that all good things must come to an end. And in that end, if I believed I would hurt Dallas more than I could help him, I'd let him go.

In that moment, I realized how very much I loved him.

CHAPTER 8
A BRAVE FACE

I WAS DRESSED AND READY TO GO. BRIA HAD CHOSEN A long, dark-green gown and a matching coat. Emerald earrings twinkled at my ears. But although my dress and jewels were lovely, unease gnawed at me. My maids didn't have details about what my visit would entail. I wrinkled my nose as I watched them, my nerves thrumming. "Are you excited to see your family?" Bettina asked, sensing my unease.

"I can't wait." My face relaxed into a smile. "I miss them so much."

"I'm sure they're thrilled, too." Evangeline grinned as she finished with my luggage. "I hope you have a lovely trip."

"I hope you show that Tamara who the real front-runner is." Bria put her hands on her hips. "She's been bragging nonstop since she got back. She has her maids convinced that she's getting a proposal. Well, I told them a thing or two—"

"Bria," Evangeline interrupted gently, "let's not make Miss West nervous."

Bria *harrumphed*. "Fine." She started smoothing my hair with renewed vigor.

I heard a knock on the door. "The car is ready for Miss West," the sentinel announced.

"Have a wonderful time, miss." Evangeline surprised me with a hug.

The twins followed suit, squeezing me tightly. "We're rooting for you," Bettina said.

Bria held me close and whispered in my ear. "Please crush Tamara's bragging black soul for me."

I giggled as she released me. "I'll see what I can do."

The sentinels brought my bags, and we met Dallas, Mira Kinney, and the film crew on the front lawn. Dallas smiled at me as Mira smoothed her outfit, getting ready for filming. This morning the television host wore a shiny, fitted black pantsuit and sky-high black patent-leather heels. She smiled, almost blinding me with her white teeth, as I joined them. "Miss West. It's a pleasure to see you again."

"Thank you, Mira. It's nice to see you, too."

She leaned toward me and adjusted the collar of my coat. "I hope this visit is a rousing success, even better than Miss Layne's. Knock 'em dead."

"Th-thank you." I swallowed hard, willing myself to be brave.

Mira organized the film crew while Dallas clasped my hand and beamed at me, resplendent in his ceremonial uniform. "Hello again."

I cleared my throat primly. "Your Highness."

His eyes sparkled in the sunlight, and he squeezed my hand. "I am looking forward to our visit. I'll be very happy to see your family again, under better circumstances."

Last time we'd traveled to Settlement 4, my sister had been ill with a high fever. Dallas had saved her life by sending a top-notch pediatrician and the medicine Winnie needed to get better.

I smiled at him. "Me, too."

"I am especially looking forward to having you all to myself."

I coughed, my cheeks heating furiously. "Yes. Quite."

Dallas chuckled darkly, sending all sorts of feels through me, as Mira snapped her fingers for the lights. She turned toward us, microphone in hand. "We're here with His Royal Highness and Miss Gwyneth West, one of our four finalists, as they get ready to leave for their overnight trip to Settlement Four. Your Highness, what are you most looking forward to on this visit?"

Dallas smiled for the camera. "I am greatly looking forward to spending more time in Settlement Four, getting to know its citizens better during this quick trip. I am also honored to get to see Miss West's family again, who I came to care for very much during our last visit to Four. But most of all, I am honored"—he put his arm around my shoulders and pulled me against him—"to spend time with Miss West. She always inspires me. I hope the audience has the opportunity to get to know her better, to see how amazing she really is."

Mira Kinney put a hand over her heart as I leaned back into Dallas for support. "That's quite the compliment, Your Highness."

He smiled at her—handsome, dashing, and utterly charming—and I imagined a hundred thousand women fanning themselves at home. "I consider it a compliment that Miss West said yes to staying as a finalist."

Mira arched an eyebrow and turned to face the cameras. "You heard it here first, settlers! Now sit back, relax, and enjoy the ride to Four. We'll be with His Highness and Miss West for every second of this journey. Stay tuned." She turned off her microphone and motioned to the cameramen. "That's a wrap!"

She nodded toward Dallas. "That's quite the statement you just made."

His smile vanished, replaced quickly with a frown. "I thought that since you forced Gwyneth into that provocative dress and had her crash my date with Miss Iman, I might help rehabilitate her image."

A few weeks ago, Mira and Tariq had had me interrupt Dallas's date with Shaye to increase drama on the show. In the end, it made me look petty and jealous, wearing a too-tight dress while poaching on my friend's time with the prince.

Mira frowned. "I told you—that was Tariq's idea, not mine."

"You've known me long enough to know I wouldn't have approved."

Mira bristled, then sighed. "You're right. It was the

wrong decision. But trust me, I'm in Miss West's corner. It doesn't matter what anyone else says."

Dallas's big body went tense. "Excuse me?"

She reached out and clasped his arm. "This show is about engaging the audience as they watch you fall in love with one of the contestants. All the stunts and clever editing in the world can't hide the truth. Make the most of this visit, Your Highness. Show the world who Miss West really is and why you care for her. This is your opportunity for the audience to see her through your eyes. Use every second."

He took her measure, then nodded. "I will, Mira. Thank you."

"I'm sorry about your date with Miss Iman. Can you forgive me?"

He bowed. "You are forgiven. Now, let's go. As you said, every second is precious."

He held out his hand for me, and we headed to the waiting SUV, the same one we'd driven to Settlement 4 the first time. I had happy memories from the time we'd spent in the backseat of that car, but my heart pounded in anticipation. *Use every second.* Mira's words thrummed through me, along with a spike of adrenaline.

Dallas leaned closer, keeping his voice down. "The cameras will be with us for the entire ride, as well as the rest of the visit—at least, until I can convince Mira to give us some peace. I want you to follow my lead and to trust me. I watched the footage of my visit with Tamara, and I understand why Tariq hailed it a 'massive success.' But we're going to do better than that. We are going to be honest, and we are going to show the people of the settlements what we would be like as rulers. Are you with me?"

"Yes." I breathlessly followed him into the backseat of the giant vehicle. But there was no respite inside; three tiny cameras were strategically positioned around the interior of the car, all the better to track our every move.

Plastering on my game face, I smiled for the cameras. But I worried. Would the next twenty-four hours be enough to help me win not only the prince's favor—but also the favor of all the settlements?

WE DROVE FOR AN HOUR, SPEEDILY HEADING FOR Settlement 4, a long procession of vehicles stretching before and after us. Black Guardsmen in massive SUVs led the motorcade. Mira and the production crew drove directly behind us, followed closely by several cars filled with more Black Guardsmen. "We'll make quite the entrance," I joked.

"It'll certainly be a spectacle—and Mira will love that." Dallas smiled. "It's good for the settlements, too. It brings excitement and unity to have royal visits. My family hasn't visited enough. I plan to change that."

"I think that's wonderful. I remember how excited my neighbors were when we were here the last time." Crowds had lined the street to catch a glimpse of the prince, cheering as we drove past.

Mindful of the cameras, Dallas continued small talk, leading me through an easy conversation about the weather and my favorite foods at the palace. But then his expression turned serious, and he reached for my hand. "Gwyneth, tell me more about your family."

My breath caught in my throat. "As you know, my younger brother and sister live with my mother. She's homeschooling them at the moment." I left out the fact that their private school had long since shut its doors, per order of the king. In our present financial condition, we wouldn't have been able to afford it, anyway.

"And what of the rest of your family?" Dallas's gaze burned into mine, and my jaw dropped.

"I'm sorry?" Was he asking me what I thought he was asking me?

"What of your father? You never mention him."

"I... Um..."

He reached for my hands. "Miss West, neither you nor many of the other girls from the contest ever mention your father or older brothers."

"Yes, well," I stammered.

Dallas's eyes flashed with sympathy and kindness. "That's because you've been afraid. But you needn't be, and neither should the other contestants or any of our citizens. I know about these family members, the men that no one dare speak about. They're dead, or still fighting a war that they haven't given up on. They're rebels. I met so many young women who came to the palace with fear in their hearts, fear they'd be discovered as rebel sympathizers simply because the people they loved had fought for their country. I want to tell you—you personally, Miss West, as well as the people at home watching—I don't judge you. Any of you. Each one of us would fight to protect our home. The settlers didn't know my family or what we represented when we came down from the North. And for that, I owe every settler an apology."

I swallowed hard, completely taken aback by his directness. But underneath my surprise, fear lurked. *The king will not stand for this sort of talk.* "Your Highness. Th-thank you."

He gripped my hands tighter. "You do not need to thank me for doing what's right. That's my duty and my honor as Crown Prince of the Settlements. I believe that you and I can work together to bring peace, real peace, to the settlements. You understand what people have gone through, as you've lived through it yourself. Together, we can unite the settlements as one prosperous, happy nation. Do you agree?"

I nodded, momentarily unable to speak.

"Good." Dallas seemed to calm down and sat back against his seat. "We are heading to a new government building in Settlement Four. It's a community outreach center. I was inspired by our first visit to your settlement, Miss West. I want to provide services that have been sorely lacking in the past few years, since the revolution."

I finally found my voice. "That's very generous, Your Highness. What sort of services do you mean?"

"Basic services to promote the health and wellness of the citizens of Four." Dallas watched the countryside fly by. "A medical clinic, like we discussed, so that people can get the attention they need. A pharmacy. A tutoring center for children and a skills clinic for adults who wish to continue their education. And counseling services so that citizens can get the help they need to deal with the loss of loved ones—rebels and non-rebels alike."

I squeezed his hand. "I think that's a wonderful idea. I know for a fact that resources are in short supply in Four."

He nodded. "We will visit the clinic this afternoon, then dine with your family. I'll be holding a meeting with citizens tomorrow morning, to discuss the center and any concerns people have. Will you help me, Gwyneth? Will you be there and talk about your experience with the royal family? There's been so much mystery surrounding us. I want that to end."

I nodded, even as icy needles jabbed my spine. *Is Dallas talking about outing himself as a vampire?* The king wanted to continue to hide his family's ancestry, but Dallas did not. We were being filmed, but as far as I knew, no one could see this footage yet except for the production crew.

Did the prince plan to tell the citizens of Settlement 4 the truth about being a vampire? What was Dallas playing at? Was he really making this bold a move?

Leery of the three cameras pointed our way, I didn't dare ask him. I just held onto his hand for dear life, praying that he knew what he was doing.

CHAPTER 9
WARM WELCOMES

WE KEPT THE CONVERSATION NEUTRAL FOR THE REST of the car ride. With the cameras present, we couldn't discuss his plans in detail. A snog-fest was also out of the question.

I knew Tamara would disagree, but I was no Tamara.

Still, we held hands for the entire ride. Being so close to Dallas was a relief—I wasn't going to lie to myself. There was no place I'd rather be. He reached for me, pulling me closer as we arrived in Settlement 4 and drove slowly toward the downtown district. I snuggled against his broad chest as we looked out the windows to the streets, which were lined with cheering fans holding signs.

"Choose Gwyn!" one read.

"Dallas + Gwyn 4Eva!" read another.

Two young girls held another large sign, decorated with glitter, hearts, and flowers: "4 Welcomes the Prince!"

The prince leaned forward and lowered the privacy screen. "Can you pull over?"

The driver nodded. He hit a button on his dashboard as he slowed and pulled toward the curb. "His Highness would like to stop for a moment."

A crackling noise issued from the speakers. "Copy that." The vehicles in front and behind us slowed, then we all stopped.

Dallas turned to me, his eyes sparkling. "Shall we?"

I grinned. "I'd love to." I might have been a bit shy, but these were my people. I wanted the chance to show how wonderful the prince truly was.

He reached for my hand, and together, we climbed out of the car into the sunny, pleasant early afternoon. The wind was still a bit brisk, but I wrapped my coat around me and enjoyed the sun on my face and the smiles and cheers from the onlookers.

Was it just this morning I saw my brother? With the sun, and the smiling, and Dallas's hand clasped firmly around mine, it seemed a year ago.

"Your Highness!" one young woman screeched. "Oh my goodness, he's here! He's real!"

"And he's *gorgeous!*" her friend announced, causing Dallas to chuckle.

He bowed to the young ladies as their jaws went slack. "It's a pleasure to meet you," he said, grinning widely. "Thank you for having me to your lovely settlement."

"Uh..." one girl said.

"Ah..." said the other.

Dallas passed on to the next group, and I winked at the girls. "He has that effect on people. I get it."

They giggled, their cheeks reddening. "We're rooting for you," one said breathlessly. "Become the princess, Gwyn. Bring glory and honor back to Four."

I curtsied, my own cheeks flaming. "I shall do my best. You have my word."

Black Guardsmen followed us as we worked our way through the crowd. The sentinels fanned out on either side, but instead of being menacing, they smiled at the crowd. Still, I knew they were searching for any potential threats. Fine with me.

Mira moved lightning fast, setting up a shot with the crowd cheering behind her. She grinned at the onlookers. "Are you excited for the prince's visit?"

"Yes!" the crowd roared back.

Dallas laughed as he shook hands and signed autographs. Several girls visibly swooned as they got close to him, and I didn't blame them. Tall and handsome, his pale skin brilliant in the sunlight, Dallas was a vision. I sighed as I watched him shake another hand, greedily wishing he'd put his hands on me instead.

"You're *besotted*," a familiar voice said.

I looked up to see Lyra, tall and poised as ever, grinning at me. "Lyra!" I reached for my old friend and pulled her in for a hug. "I'm so glad you're here."

She giggled against me, then pulled back and showed me her sign: "Gwyneth for Princess!" It was covered with rainbow glitter and star stickers.

"Aw, you shouldn't have."

Lyra swatted me. "Are you crazy? We're all so excited we can barely contain ourselves! It's all anyone talks about."

Dallas drew farther away, and I squeezed my friend's hand. "It's good to see you. I miss you."

"Don't come home on my account." She laughed. "I'll come visit you at the palace when you're the princess."

Dallas was suddenly beside me. Lyra's dark-brown eyes almost popped out of her head as she took him in, his tall, muscular form, ceremonial uniform, loads of thick hair, and disarmingly handsome face.

He bowed to her, then smiled charmingly when he rose. "Hello."

"Your Highness." Lyra, typically unflappable, sounded breathless.

I grinned at them. "Your Highness, this is my friend Miss Lyra Thornton. Miss Thornton, this is obviously the prince."

He took her hand and kissed it. "It's a pleasure, Miss Thornton."

Lyra looked as if she might need to fan herself. "The pleasure is mine. Really."

Dallas nodded to me. "We must make our way down the street and then back to the car if we want to make it to the center on time."

"Of course."

Dallas grabbed my hand, lacing my fingers through his, a move not lost on Lyra. She grinned at us. "It was lovely to see you both."

Dallas nodded. "We'll meet again, I'm certain."

He turned away, and Lyra gaped at me. *Oh my God!* she mouthed. *He's perfection!*

All I could do was giggle in response.

The prince and I continued down the street, shaking hands, hugging children, and signing autographs as the cameras captured every second. For once, I was thankful for them. Dallas's smile for the gathered crowd was genuine. In return, their enthusiasm and excitement about our visit was infectious.

He held my hand in broad daylight, and even though we were in the midst of an excited crowd, I felt calm and safe. It was as if Dallas's hold anchored me to the shore, so I was no longer adrift in my emotions. But I knew the undertow was out there, lurking, waiting to drag me under.

I had to have faith and hope we could both hold on.

❦

"THIS IS AMAZING." I STARED UP AT THE COMMUNITY center. The government had refurbished one of the downtown federal buildings to its former splendor. The gleaming brick facade was elegant, and the repaired clock tower and spire jutted gracefully into the sky.

Dallas smiled, inspecting the large building. "They've done a good job. Come, let's go see inside."

Hand in hand, followed closely by Mira Kinney and a team of Black Guardsmen, we entered the building. I admired the marble flooring and the grand staircase, the ornate carvings in wood painted baby blue, and the soaring windows.

A large staff waited for us in the lobby. They bowed and curtsied as a royal sentinel announced the prince. Dallas introduced me to the employees, telling me what their roles were. Every one of them clutched my hand. One woman leaned in and whispered in my ear, "Thank you for this, Miss West. The center is a blessing. We're going to do wonderful things here, and it's all because of you."

I clasped her hand. "It was completely His Highness's idea. I cannot take credit."

"But you must." The woman smiled, a web of glorious wrinkles breaking out over her face. "You were the spark that lit the flame."

I nodded, my cheeks heating. I wasn't used to being treated like, well, like royalty, but each person I met spoke to me with a reverence that I was completely unaccustomed to. We reached the end of the line, and Dallas clasped my hand once more. "I'd like to show you the clinic. It's down the hall." He seemed quiet all of a sudden, almost as if he were holding his breath. Mira excitedly whispered directions to the camera crew, and they hustled down the corridor to set up the shot.

"What's all the fuss about?" I asked.

Dallas looked straight ahead. "I don't know." But it sounded like a lie.

Curious, I clutched his hand as we walked through the center. But I understood why he was tense as soon as we reached our destination, a set of double doors with a gleaming gold sign above it: "The West Medical Clinic." The cameras got closer, their klieg lights in our faces, scrutinizing my reaction. I put my hand over my heart, gaping back and forth between the sign and the prince. "You named the clinic after my family?"

Dallas nodded, looking unsure. "I wanted to honor your family for their bravery—for weathering the storm without your father, for keeping the faith when Winifred was sick, for sending you to the competition in the hope of a brighter future. I believe your family's spirit shows the essence of Settlement Four and all the lovely people here."

My eyes filled with happy tears. "Oh, Dallas. That's incredible."

He reached for me. "You don't mind?"

I threw myself into his arms, cameras be damned. "Are you kidding? I'm beyond honored!" I hugged him fiercely.

He hugged me back, gently kissing my hair. It took us a moment to remember that we were surrounded by Mira Kinney, the film crew, and many guards. We both coughed as we pulled away. "Er, sorry about that." I looked sheepishly at Dallas.

His eyes sparkled. "I'm not."

"Neither am I," Mira said gleefully. "This is so exciting! It's such an honor, Miss West. I'm thrilled for your family. Your Highness, your thoughtfulness and generosity never cease to amaze me. Let's take a tour of the clinic, shall we, and show the audience the good work that's happening here?"

The sentinels opened the doors, and we headed inside. I sucked in a deep breath as I peered around—this was more than a clinic. It looked like a brand-new wing of a top hospital. Pristine beds lined the wall, doctors and nurses bustling between the rows to check on patients. From across the room, I recognized Dr. Cameron's pretty face, her dark skin and braids. She was the one who'd saved Winnie.

Dr. Cameron saw us and came over immediately. "Your Highness, Miss West. It's a pleasure." She curtsied, which looked funny because she was wearing scrubs and a lab coat. "I hope you enjoy what you see here at the West Clinic. We've had an amazing response from the citizens of Four. People are telling me we're saving lives."

"How long have you been open?" I asked.

"Just a few days, but we already have a waiting list."

Dallas frowned. "How many?"

Dr. Cameron checked her clipboard. "Two hundred twenty-three as of right now."

"Double your staff and get those patients in here," Dallas ordered.

Dr. Cameron's face lit up. "Yes, Your Highness!" She took us on a quick tour of the facility, showing us the top-of-the-line equipment they'd assembled. I was no medical expert, but it was clear that no expense had been spared in setting up the clinic. "We can do vaccinations, screen for cancer and other illnesses, and really accomplish something on the preventative side. We're also fully equipped for emergency medical treatments. This is going to change the lives of the citizens of Four."

Dallas beamed at her. "I'm so impressed that you were able to pull this together so quickly."

Dr. Cameron smiled. "Having funding makes all the difference, Your Highness. We've been able to work a miracle."

He shook her hand. "I can't wait for you to do this for all the settlements."

Her smile widened. "Are we going to?"

"Yes, we are. And together, we're going to strengthen this nation."

She looked back and forth between us, joy lighting up her face. "I knew good things were coming. I never doubted."

Dallas bowed. "Your loyalty means everything to me, Dr. Cameron."

She couldn't stop smiling. "What are your plans for the rest of the afternoon?"

"We'd like to visit the children's wing for a while, if that's acceptable to you."

Dr. Cameron's eyes sparkled. "You're going to make their day, Your Highness. They're beside themselves with excitement."

We followed Dr. Cameron to another room, and I leaned close to Dallas. "There's a whole children's wing?"

He nodded. "They're the most vulnerable. We have to protect them."

Something about the way his voice got husky when talking about kids made my insides go positively squishy. Bloody hell, Lyra was right. I *was* besotted.

We reached the wing, and another sign had me

clutching my heart: "The Winifred West Children's Wing."

"Dallas. My sister is going to be beside herself with excitement."

He grinned, clearly pleased. "She's my favorite patient. She deserves a little recognition."

I couldn't wait to see my sister. She would never stop bragging, but it was so worth it.

Dr. Cameron got ready to open the door. "Be prepared." She chuckled. "They're going to go ballistic." Mira Kinney made sure the crew had a clean shot, and the doctor opened the door. The room was enormous, filled with at least fifty occupied hospital beds. The children—some of them hooked up to IVs, others with masks over their faces—clapped and hollered when they saw us. They cheered and gleefully threw balloons into the air. "Welcome Prince Black and Miss West," a clearly handmade banner read. The words were written in a mixture of crayon and Magic Marker.

Dallas and I grinned at the sea of excited faces, then at each other. "Shall we?" he asked.

I nodded, reaching for his hand. I had only one answer. "Yes."

CHAPTER 10
FORMER GLORY

AFTER A FULL AFTERNOON VISITING WITH THE children and getting to know more about the center, Dallas and I returned to the motorcade. We climbed inside the SUV. "Where are we going next?" I asked.

He looked straight ahead, a sign I'd come to understand meant he was slightly embarrassed about something. "Our hotel."

I almost choked; it came out a spluttering cough. "I'm sorry?"

He cleared his throat. "We're going to our hotel to change before dinner with your family."

"But Dallas, there aren't hotels in Four anymore. The last one closed its doors a long time ago."

He glanced at me briefly, then turned away again. "We had one refurbished."

I arched an eyebrow. "You had an entire *hotel* refurbished for this visit?"

He nodded almost imperceptibly. "We didn't have

enough time to complete the whole project, so my team concentrated on the lobby and the first floor of suites. The rest of the hotel has been sealed off, and work will continue after we leave. But I've heard they've made quite astonishing progress. We'll be able to dine in the lobby restaurant tonight."

I was rendered speechless, which was how I remained for the rest of the short drive downtown. I stared out the window at my settlement. It appeared much improved since my last visit. Green grass grew in the parks, the sidewalks had been swept, and bright flowers bloomed in large pots on every street corner. Twinkle lights were strung between the lampposts. The atmosphere was colorful, clean, and positively festive. I turned to Dallas. "Did you refurbish the entire downtown?"

He coughed. "Yes."

I would've ribbed him about this, but the car pulled over in front of what had been the most exclusive grand hotel in Settlement 4. Since the war, it had fallen to ruin, with only stray dogs and rats as guests. But now it sparkled like new, surpassing even its former glory. I stared up at the building, which in the old America had been a bank. It was made of smooth, light-gray stone with majestic columns lining its edifice. Its large dome rose toward the sky. In the fading afternoon light, the sun glowed from behind the building. It looked as though it had a halo, a patina of glory and second chances.

Dallas was already on the sidewalk, opening the door for me, as the camera crews followed our every move.

That didn't stop me from peering up at the hotel. I couldn't help myself. "This is astonishing."

He grinned. "I've heard the inside's even more impressive."

He took my hand and led me inside. Sentinels bowed and held the doors for us. I'd thought I was done with heart clutching for one day, but I was wrong. My hand went directly heart center again as we entered the luxurious lobby. The ceiling soared to the dome, skylights flooding the large space with air and light. The marble columns were visible inside the lobby, lending an air of opulence and elegance I'd previously experienced only at the castle. Couches, chairs, and modern lamps adorned the sitting areas. In the center of the lobby, a large ornate fireplace crackled with a robust fire.

"Dallas, won't all of this go to waste?" The people in 4 couldn't afford such luxuries.

"Eventually, I'm hoping our economy is restored so that grand hotels like this one become useful again. In the interim, I thought that the royal family and its representatives could stay here when we're visiting Four."

I arched an eyebrow. "Are you planning on coming here often?"

"I certainly hope so." He coughed. "In any event, I thought it a terrible waste that such a beautiful building was crumbling in the middle of your hometown. I had to do something."

Touched, I drew closer to his side. He took my hand as he gazed at the spacious lobby. "My main architect said this was an impossible project. I fired him on the spot."

"Why?"

"Because I saw the glory inside the ruin. What he saw as unobtainable, I saw as natural. It all depends on your mindset, Gwyneth. Whether you think something is impossible or you think you can do it, you are setting yourself up for either failure or success."

"Are you still talking about the lobby?" I teased. "Or are you being generally philosophical?"

He kissed my forehead. "Actually, I was talking about us."

Emotion welled up inside me, but two sentinels came forward. "Sorry to interrupt, Your Highness, but your guests will be here soon. Your rooms are ready. We can see you upstairs."

"Thank you." We headed through the lobby to a grand, sweeping staircase. We climbed, with Mira and her team following closely. I realized that she'd been quietly but fastidiously recording our every move, our every touch. Perhaps she'd wanted to fade into the background so the prince and I acted more naturally.

Blushing, I realized she'd succeeded. The prince and I hadn't kept our hands off each other for a moment. I'd been calling him "Dallas" for the entire trip. He'd named a medical clinic after my family, and an entire wing after my baby sister. In one week, he'd refurbished a hotel, not to mention the downtown of my city, in preparation for this visit.

I supposed the proverbial cat was out of the bag.

I didn't know what anyone—the audience, the royal family, the other remaining contestants—would make of our attachment. I resolved not to care for the next twenty-four hours, until I was back at the castle and in the thick of the competition.

We reached the landing, and the sentinels took us to a room. "Here we are, Your Majesty." I waited politely as they opened the door and Dallas swept through.

The sentinels didn't blink, but Dallas stuck his head out a moment later. "Gwyneth? Aren't you coming?"

"Uh... I..." I looked around, my gaze locking with Mira Kinney's. She said nothing, just smiling as the cameras rolled, capturing my befuddlement and quickly heating cheeks. I turned back to Dallas. "Where's my room?"

He chuckled. "It's through here. We have an adjoining suite, but I assure you, you have your own room. You can have all the privacy you'd like. I thought we'd enjoy the view together." His eyes sparkled.

"Th-thank you." Nerves jangling, I stepped into the suite, the camera crew hot on my trail. The spacious room was luxurious, like the lobby, with crystal chandeliers, thick carpets, and fresh flowers in brightly colored vases. But the suite's quiet elegance made it more comfortable than regal. The view from the floor-to-ceiling windows was of the entire downtown. The formerly bustling space now held empty but still glorious skyscrapers, parking garages, restaurants, and parks. It was empty, but with the fairy lights winking below and the green grass visible from the park, hope soared in my heart that my city could one day be restored. "It's a beautiful view."

I looked up to find Dallas staring at me. "Indeed. It's quite my favorite."

We both went back to looking out the window.

"Your family will be here soon," Dallas said a minute later. "We should get ready."

I smiled, then remembering the cameras for once, I curtsied. "Your Highness. I'll see you shortly."

His gaze burned into mine as he reached for my hand. "I know it's only for a little while, but it's still too long."

My cheeks flamed. I knew exactly what he meant. "I'll be quick." I kissed him then swiftly turned away before the cameras could catch the longing on my face.

MY ROOM—WHICH HAD A LOCK ON THE DOOR, I noticed—was similarly spectacular, with an enormous four-poster bed and original artwork on the walls. Still, I barely glimpsed it. I was eager to get back to Dallas, and excitement bubbled inside me at the thought of seeing my family. The sentinels had carefully unpacked my clothes. My gown hung neatly in the closet. But I panicked as I took the fine lavender material between my fingers. I missed Evangeline, Bria, and Bettina. *How on earth will I do my hair?*

A knock jarred me from my reverie. "Yes?"

Mira Kinney opened the door a crack and smiled through. "Can I send in my hair and makeup team? Your maids threatened them before we left. They said they'd mutiny if we let you on camera with a messy bun and no makeup." She chuckled.

I sighed in relief. "Yes, please. I've become quite spoiled, I'm afraid. I'm completely ruined when it comes to doing my own hair."

She chuckled. "I understand. Actually, Gwyneth, may we speak for a moment? Off the record?"

I immediately became wary. "Of course. Come in."

"Thanks." Mira closed the door behind her and sat at the edge of a wingback chair. "You know I went to Eleven with the Prince and Miss Layne."

I nodded. "Go on."

"This trip doesn't compare."

My stomach dropped. "I see."

"No, no, don't misunderstand me, Gwyneth. I meant that as a compliment. Your relationship with the prince is light-years ahead of what he has with Tamara. You and His Majesty are in another galaxy, one she has no chance of visiting. And I've observed him with the other girls, too. I don't see the same sort of connection to either of them, not at all."

I twisted a lock of my hair. "I'd say thank you, but I have a feeling there's about to be a 'but.'"

She smiled. "Clever girl. Of course there is."

"Go on."

"The king asked to see the tape when we returned from Eleven. I watched it with him. He had a lot of questions about Tamara's parents—their charity work, their influence, their friends. He was quite interested in their particulars."

I sighed. "I understand. Tamara is an advantageous match for the prince, and I am not."

Mira smoothed her hair back from her face. "I disagree. From an editorial perspective, I find your connection to His Highness more compelling, which translates to better ratings. You two are star-crossed lovers."

I wrinkled my nose. "What does that mean, exactly?"

"It means you are not favored by the stars."

I sank onto the bed. "I don't want that to be true and yet..."

"And yet, you are a clever girl." Mira smiled at me. "The king wants Tamara as the princess because he wants her family money and connections. But I see a larger picture here, one that stars *you* as the savior of the settlements."

I blinked at her. "How so?"

Mira patted my hand. "I've done some digging into you—more than that slick and eely Tariq ever did before he brought you to the palace. I know about your family, Gwyneth. I know who they are."

I didn't dare ask if she knew my brother was currently a resident in the castle dungeons. I felt as if I might break into hives and vaguely wondered if they could be covered by makeup.

"Hey. You don't have to worry about me," Mira said. "I'm here to frame the narrative, not to hijack it. And I believe, much like the prince, that the audience wants someone like you to win. You're relatable. People understand what you've been through, because they've lost loved ones to the revolution too. So that's what I wanted to say—you have to be brave. You have to be a bit more balls-out, if you'll pardon the expression."

I coughed. "What do you mean?"

She looked me directly in the eye. "If the prince asks you about your father on camera again, you should tell the truth."

"The king will see me hanged." My voice came out thick.

"The prince won't let that happen. You know he'll protect you."

"Why are you telling me to do this?"

She smiled. "For ratings. At the heart of this, that's what I care about."

I groaned. "Bloody hell, Mira."

"But I care about you, too. And I've come to care deeply for the people in the settlements. We could all have a bright future here, but we need each other to make it happen. The revolution isn't over yet, and you're uniquely situated to unite the settlements. And I want to be the one to film it. We can help make each other's stars rise. Just think about it." She stood as if prepared to go. "I'll send in hair and makeup. His Highness doesn't look like he can bear being away from you, so I'll tell them to be quick."

"Thank you."

But as she left, I wondered, should I really be thanking Mira Kinney? Or should I run, screaming, in the other direction?

I WANTED TO TALK TO DALLAS ABOUT MY conversation with Mira, but there was no time. Hair and makeup whipped me into shape, zipped me into my pretty lavender gown, and sent me to the prince's suite before I even had a chance to fully process what she'd said.

Star-crossed lovers.

Tell the truth.

Unite the settlements.

Bloody hell. Wasn't the Pageant a dating competition? Instead, I was embroiled in politics that could result in my head on a spike, adorning the king's view from his private study.

I hoped we'd have champagne at dinner.

"Gwyneth, you're stunning." Dallas beamed at me as I hustled into his suite.

No matter what else was happening, the sight of him made my heart swell. In his black ceremonial uniform and deep-purple cape, he was so tall and handsome it almost hurt to look at him. Remembering myself, I curtsied. "Your Highness. You're looking dashing, as usual."

He chuckled as he held out his arm for me. "Your maids will approve of your hair, I believe. It looks lovely." Mira's team had worked quickly to arrange my long hair into an elaborate updo, replete with tiny bobby pins adorned with jewels. "You're sparkling."

"Winnie will appreciate that." I grinned, pushing my worries about what Mira had said to the back of my mind. I couldn't wait to see my family.

"I've had word they're waiting for us downstairs." We left the suite, followed by the camera crew, and descended the grand staircase. I saw my mother, brother, and sister in the lobby below, admiring the hotel and chatting with Mira Kinney. With the prince at my side, the stars winking through the skylights, the roaring fire, and my family so close, my heart soared.

Dallas stole a glance at me. "You're radiant."

I smiled, my heart full. "I'm very blessed. No matter what happens, I'll keep this moment in my heart as a happy memory."

He squeezed my arm. "It's just the beginning."

My sister caught sight of me and clapped. "Gwyn!"

At that, I moved as fast as I could without breaking my neck to get to her. "Winnie!" I wrapped her in a hug and twirled her around, her pretty little ball gown ballooning around her. I kissed her cheeks, careful not to smudge the hint of sparkling pink blush—Mother must've allowed her a bit of makeup.

"Let go," she whispered against my chest. "I've got to curtsy for His Majesty."

Her solemn tone made me giggle. "Yes, of course." She curtsied perfectly for Dallas while I gathered my brother in my arms, peppering him with kisses. "Hello, Remy! There's a good boy. I've missed you so much!" He squirmed beneath my grasp, but I didn't let go until I'd kissed him and told him I loved him a hundred more times.

"Let *go*," he groaned. "I've got to see the prince!" As soon as I released him, he went to Dallas. The prince grinned down at him, then they did some elaborate hand-shake that Remy had taught him the last time we'd visited.

"Hello, my dear." My mother was suddenly beside me, pulling me in for a formal hug that rumpled neither of us.

"Mother." I squeezed her back, careful of her dress.

"I think they like him." My mother smiled as we watched Dallas with my brother and sister.

"What gave it away?" I snorted, feeling left out as Winnie and Remy fawned over Dallas as though he were the Easter Bunny. "I didn't get a curtsy or a special handshake."

"They're so excited over this. They've spoken of nothing else for days." My mother chuckled, then shrewdly looked me over. "You look well, Gwyneth."

Checking that the cameras were focused on the prince and not us, I pursed my lips. "An endless supply of healthy, delicious food, luxury clothing, and a whole hair-and-makeup team will do that for you."

She arched an eyebrow, and I noticed that her auburn hair was expertly smoothed, and her own makeup was flawless. She was wearing a brand-new gown, dark blue with gold brocade adorning the front. "Speaking of looking good."

She shrugged prettily. "His Highness sent a team for us. I could get used to this, you know. I'd *like* to get used to it."

I sighed. "I've no idea what's going to happen, Mother."

She *tsked*. "He's refurbishing an entire city for you. Have some self-confidence, child. I raised you better than that. "

I looked at her again, her elegant features set off by the professional makeup. And then to my horror, I remembered Balkyn, starving and sunken-eyed in the dungeon of the palace. I reached for her hand and squeezed it. "Oh, Mother. You have no idea what I'm up against." I couldn't tell her about my brother, and I refused to tell her I'd learned that my father was at large and very ill. Neither of us could do anything about it at the moment except worry, and I vowed to protect her from that. The less she knew, the safer she was.

"What's the matter?" A veteran mom, she knew how to keep her voice low enough not be overheard.

"I can't tell you."

She gave me a sharp look. "Is this about our family? The episode with that other girl—the one from Eleven— was all about her parents and their support for the royals. I knew it meant trouble for us."

I shook my head. "It might end up being all right. But I don't know yet."

"I wish the war had never happened. I wish they'd never left us." Years of practice kept my mother's eyes dry and clear, her back straight. You'd never know that, inside, her heart was broken.

I reached for her hand and squeezed it. "I wish that, too."

Trumpets sounded, and half a dozen white-liveried servers came to the lobby. They bowed with a flourish. "Dinner is served." Delicious smells wafted from the dining room.

Winnie and Remy followed the waiters, skipping, and Dallas warmly greeted my mother. He offered her his arm and clasped my hand, too, and I was reminded of our walk with the queen. It was a funny feeling, having us all together. It seemed right, somehow. As if we all belonged together.

My heart would've been light, and this would've been perfect, but the delicious meal awaiting us and the happiness of being reunited with my family served only to remind me of our missing pieces, my father and brother, who were alone and without.

But I was my mother's daughter. I put on a brave face and smiled for the prince, my family, and the cameras. You'd never know that inside, my heart was also broken.

"I'M STUFFED," REMY GROANED, THEN HELD UP HIS

hands to the prince. "Carry me? My stomach's too heavy —I can't walk."

Laughing, Dallas hoisted him and carried him through the lobby. We'd feasted on crab cakes, beef tenderloin, kale with lemon, and for dessert, cupcakes and chocolate cream pie. I could barely walk myself.

I caught Winnie frowning at them and knew she was jealous. "C'mere. I'll carry you to the car. *And* we'll win."

"It's not a race," Dallas protested. But I didn't listen. I quickly stepped out of my heels, grabbed Winnie, threw her into a piggyback position, and ran to the car. Winnie giggled the whole time and pumped her fist when we got there first. We tucked my siblings into the waiting car, a sentinel behind the wheel, and I kissed each of them. Dallas and Remy did their fist bump. Then the prince kissed both my mother and Winnie's hands. "Thank you for a lovely evening."

My mother beamed. "Your Highness, your kindness knows no bounds. We are honored to dine with you. I daresay I even approve of leaving you with my daughter overnight." We'd offered them a suite, but it was late, and my mother wanted Winnie and Remy to get a good night's sleep in their own beds. We were meeting again in the morning for a ribbon-cutting ceremony at the clinic.

He coughed. "I will keep her safe, my lady, and I will protect her honor."

She smiled at him. "I know you will."

They drove off into the night, and Dallas reached for my hand. "It's late." My heart rate kicked up as I nodded, following him inside. I grabbed my shoes but didn't bother to put them on. Weary from the long day, we took our time climbing the stairs. Even the production crew seemed tired. They dragged their equipment along, still filming, but several of the human team were yawning. Once we reached our suite, Dallas turned to Mira, the production crew, and the sentinels. "Leave us."

Mira frowned. "Your Highness, we had an agreement—"

"And the agreement was that you could film everything except when I told you that you couldn't. I am exercising my right to privacy and a good night's sleep."

Mira crossed her arms against her chest. "With all due respect, Your Highness, you don't sleep."

He cleared his throat, undeterred. "I'm also protecting Miss West's rights. So go to bed, all of you, or at least take a break. We'll all be bloody up and back at it at the crack of dawn."

Mira's shrewd gaze flicked from the prince to me. "As you wish, Your Highness." They immediately left us, except for the sentinels who would guard our doors throughout the night.

Now I was alone with the prince, and I didn't know whether to laugh or cry.

"Come." Dallas led me into the suite, unbuttoning the top portion of his uniform. Just the brief glimpse of his chest had my heart somersaulting in a way that almost made me feel sick. He poured himself a glass of wine, then another very tiny one for me. "Here. You look like you need this."

I accepted it but set it on a nearby table. If a peek at

the prince's chest had me on the edge of a coronary, I needed to keep my wits about me.

He sank into the chair beside me. "What's wrong?"

"Uh... I guess I'm a bit nervous about being alone with you."

He shook his head. "That's not what I meant, but we can discuss that in a moment. I meant, what was wrong all through dinner? You were just going through the motions. I could tell something was troubling you."

I melted toward him. "You could tell, huh? You know me better than my own mother."

He cocked his head, as if waiting for me to go on.

"It's my brother." I sighed. "And my father. I realized tonight that I have to hide everything from my mother in order to keep her safe. Plus, what good would telling her the truth do? It would break her heart even more. But it was hard to relax and enjoy the evening simply *because* it was so wonderful. Balkyn is starving himself to death, and my father might very well be dead. It's hard to enjoy myself when others I love are suffering so much."

He reached for my hand and kissed it. "And this is why I want to be with you, Gwyneth. Because you feel things so deeply. You do not have a selfish bone in your body."

"Of course I do." I shook my head. "I stuffed myself silly with crab cakes and chocolate cream pie while my brother rots in a dungeon. I'm a hypocrite."

"You don't see yourself the way I do. I see a loving sister, a dutiful daughter, and a patriot."

I wrinkled my nose. "A patriot? How's that?"

"You were brave enough to come to the palace. You've been brave enough to weather the storm since you've been there. You've done that for your people, to give them hope."

"Dallas, I was ordered to come to the palace. And about being brave since I've been there—I rather think my survival instincts have kicked in. Fight or flight, you know." I blew out a deep breath. "While we're speaking about my role in the competition, I should tell you, Mira Kinney has a few thoughts on the topic."

Dallas had another sip of wine. "I'm sure she does."

"She wants me to be honest about my father, about my family's rebel connections. She talked to me about it earlier."

He considered me. "And what did you say?"

"I said *your* father would see me hanged."

He put down his glass. "Over my dead body."

I bit my lip. "I don't know... I don't know what to do."

"Come here." Dallas pulled me onto his lap, and heat rushed through me as he played with the delicate silk of my gown. "I don't want you to do anything that makes you uncomfortable. That being said, I have ideas about how I want to govern moving forward. Those ideas include being more honest and more inclusive of the real experience of our citizens—the *rebel* experience. Not the propaganda of my father riding in on a white horse and saving the settlements."

I swallowed hard. "I understand that, and I agree with your sentiments. But I don't want your father to hate me any more than he already does."

Dallas nodded. "I understand. Let's leave it alone, for now." His voice was soft. "Let's talk about what else is bothering you—being alone with me tonight."

"I'm not bothered." A hot blush crept up my neck. "It's just that we've never been this close together before. Unsupervised." The more I thought about it, the redder I became.

"You don't need to be nervous. As I told your mother, your virtue is safe with me."

I swallowed hard. "I know."

He tapped me under the chin, bringing my gaze to meet his. "You should go to bed now and get some rest. Tomorrow is another long day. There's a lock on your door. Use it, so that you may be comfortable."

"But I trust you one hundred percent—" I said hotly.

"It's not to lock me out." Dallas chuckled darkly. "It's so you can lock yourself in."

"Oh, you...*you...*" I spluttered, my fists clenched. "Of all the egotistical, presumptuous, cocky, conceited things I've heard... Ugh!" Red-faced, fuming, and muttering curse words, I shot up from his lap and stormed to my room.

As I locked the door, I could still hear him bloody laughing.

CHAPTER 12
IT COULD ALL BE SO SIMPLE

I STOMPED AROUND UNTIL, A MOMENT LATER, HE knocked.

I unlocked the door and glared. "What?"

Dallas looked sheepish. "I'm sorry. I was only teasing."

I arched an eyebrow. "Oh, I'm so sure."

He reached for my hand, but I pulled away.

"Gwyneth."

"What?" I had very little patience left, and I could still see the top of his pale, muscular chest. *Must. Get. A. Grip.* And not on him, although it was very tempting.

He stepped closer, and my heart did another somersault. "Please accept my apology."

I sighed. "Fine. There's some truth to it, I suppose." My gaze again flicked to the flash of his chest peeking through.

"You're not the only one who feels that way." He

came closer still, putting his hands on my hips. "May I please kiss you good night?"

His proximity—his big hands against my hips, his scent, his gaze burning into mine—undid me. I couldn't even pretend to hesitate. "Of course." I immediately sank my hands into his hair and crushed my lips against his.

He moaned and pulled me closer.

Our tongues connected, and in that moment, time stopped. A hot flash of desire, stronger than I'd ever felt, burned through me. Dallas tightened his grip on my hips, deepening the kiss, and I pressed against him.

He pulled back a moment later, his chest heaving. "Well. That was...something."

"Was?" I asked a bit desperately. "I'm quite sure we aren't finished!"

"But we have to be." He released me, looking strained. "I must be a gentleman."

"Says who?"

He chuckled but took another vexing step back. "Good night, Gwyneth. I'll see you in the morning." He took my hand and planted a chaste kiss on it.

"Fine." I frowned, a bit sourly, as he left.

He stuck his head back into the room. "You really should lock that door," he growled. "Maybe more for me than for you."

That cheered me a bit.

It took me forever to remove the bobby pins from my hair. I sighed in relief as the long waves fell around my shoulders, free from restraint. I hummed, still tingling from the kiss, as I dug through my clothes. Finally I found what Evangeline had packed for me: a pair of blush-pink silk pajamas. I put them on, brushed my teeth, and crawled into bed.

And then I sat there, wondering what Dallas was doing. I got out of bed and tiptoed to the door before knocking.

"Gwyneth?" Dallas called from the other side. "Are you knocking on your own door?"

"Yes. I didn't want to barge in on you. May I come in?"

"Of course." I found him on the couch, facing the windows and looking at the night sky. He'd changed, too, into a plain gray T-shirt and navy mesh athletic shorts. Having never seen so much of his skin before, I stopped and stared.

"Gwyneth?" He raked a hand through his hair, making it stand up in the wild spikes that I loved. "Don't you need to get some sleep?"

"Yes, well. About that. I was thinking." I stared at his biceps, barely able to form a coherent thought.

"And?" Dallas chuckled, clearly amused by my behavior.

I finally snapped out of it. "*And*, as you've vowed to protect my virtue, wouldn't it be all right if... I mean, if..."

He waited for me to go on.

"If you spent the night in my room?"

There was no more chuckling. Dallas's eyes sparkled, but he looked hesitant. "Where in your room, exactly?"

I swallowed hard. "In my bed. With me."

He sighed, a strangled sound. "Gwyneth, that's not a good idea."

"It would be okay—we could just have a sleepover." When he looked utterly lost, I continued, "Humans have their friends sleep over sometimes. You put on pajamas, have snacks—though we needn't do that," I said quickly. "And then, you know, you gossip. And fall asleep later than you should."

He arched his eyebrows, and did I imagine it, or was he blushing? "And would our sleepover involve kissing?"

"Maybe a little?" I offered, hopefully.

He chuckled. "I would love to have a sleepover with you. But I reserve the right to flee if I feel I can't behave myself."

"Fair enough." I held out my hands. "Come with me."

He followed me into my room, and we climbed into the enormous bed. I snuggled against him, thrilled to feel his bare skin with my fingertips. I lightly stroked his arms, and electricity crackled between us. It was suddenly very, very hot.

He looked at me skeptically, his eyes burning. "Is this what you normally do on a sleepover?"

"No. But I quite prefer this." I leaned up and drew him in for a long, deep kiss.

This time was different. We were in bed together, every inch of our bodies able to touch. I ran my hands down his broad chest, then his arms, my fingertips tingling from the feel of his skin. Dallas positioned himself over me and sank his hands deep into my loose hair. He deepened the kiss, and I moaned, arching my back. With his large physique, he emanated a brute, throbbing power. I clung to him, wrapping my arms around him and bringing him even closer, quite possibly in an attempt to pull him *through* me.

"Whoa, whoa." He broke the kiss, breathing hard. "I'm sorry. We have to stop."

"Why?" It was as if he was taking my favorite scone away, only a million times worse.

"Because." He raked a hand through his hair. "I can barely control myself around you, and I must."

I wanted to argue, but I knew it would only end with him lecturing me about how he'd vowed to protect my virtue and blah, blah, blah. *Virtue smirtue.* "Fine." I forced myself to sound calm and collected, the opposite of how my raging hormones felt. "Just don't leave."

"I wouldn't dream of it." He smirked at me and scooted away. "But I'll just stay over here while I collect myself. Please proceed with your gossip."

"Oh. Right." I huffed. "I don't really have any gossip, though. You know everything I know."

"What about questions, then? I know you love your questions." He was trying to appease me, but it only partially worked.

I wanted to get back to kissing, but of course, I *did* have questions. "Do you not sleep at all? Will you sit awake all night?"

"I don't sleep. I don't even rest, really—I don't find it helpful. So I usually work."

"Will you work tonight?"

"No, not tonight." His voice was husky.

"What will you do?"

His gaze raked over me. "I will watch you sleep, Gwyneth. And I will hold you, if you let me."

My body started tingling again. "Of course I'll let you. Maybe we should start now?" I asked.

He chuckled. "I need another minute. That was..." He stopped laughing, and his expression grew stormy. "I have a very intense reaction to you. I'm not accustomed to feeling like that."

I perked up a bit. "Like what?"

He frowned, a deep V forming in between his eyebrows. "Out of control. When we're kissing, I almost feel like I can't stop."

"Maybe we should try again. You know, for practice?"

He laughed. "I look forward to the day when we can practice. But it's not today."

"Have you ever..." I stumbled across the words, wanting to stop myself from asking but unable to. "Have you ever had a reaction like that before? With anyone else?" I had to know.

"Never."

I exhaled, relieved.

"Have you?"

"No, of course not."

"Have you ever had a boyfriend before?" He stared at me intensely, as if he were trying to read my mind.

"Once." My cheeks heated, thinking of the blasé and well-meaning Drew Baylor. "It wasn't serious."

Dallas sat up, puffing his chest. "Is this chap still here in Four?"

"Easy. He's no threat to you. I broke up with him months before the competition started."

"Why?"

I wrinkled my nose. "He was a bit boring, is all. I just wasn't into him."

Dallas arched an eyebrow. "Did you ever kiss him?"

I sat up. "Not the way I just kissed you, that's for sure. We barely ever touched each other. Rest easy, Your Highness."

His face softened. "Good."

I giggled. "I can't believe you're jealous over *me*. Please! You've been snogging contestants left and right. Tamara's had her chest up against you more times than I care to count."

He reached for my hand and pulled me closer. "I had to do that. It's for the show."

"I'm so sure."

He took my face in his hands. "No, Gwyneth, really. I don't want to be with anyone except you." He kissed the top of my head and settled me against his chest.

"Have you?" I asked, after a minute. "Ever had a girlfriend?"

"No."

I looked up at him. "Seriously?"

"Seriously. The Crown Prince doesn't get out much. All the young women I've known are daughters of my father's allies. I've known them all for years, so really, they're more like my cousins. The Pageant is the first chance I've had to actually date."

"Well. Huh."

He patted my back. "I know there's another question in there. Go ahead and ask it."

"So are you... Is your..." I bit my lip. "Is *your* virtue intact?"

"Yes. Very much so."

I peered up at him. "Oh."

He chuckled. "You're surprised?"

I traced a pattern on his chest, my finger skimming over the smooth cotton of his T-shirt. "You're very tall and strapping. And you seem to know what you're doing in the kissing department."

"I have no idea what I'm doing. I just know what feels good."

I bit my lip again, blushing. "That's what I'm doing, too. I think we're quite good at it."

"We are *excellent* at it." He leaned down and kissed me again, ending it too quickly. "See? A-plus."

"I'd like to study for finals," I whined.

He chuckled but stubbornly settled me back against his chest. "We will. When the time is right."

"Fine." I yawned, then tried to hide it.

"Shh, Gwyneth. You need to sleep. I'll be here all night and when you wake up."

"But I don't want to go to sleep," I mumbled. Still, the long day of traveling and excitement was catching up to me, and even though I didn't want to miss a moment with him, my eyelids drooped. "Being a human's so inconvenient sometimes."

"It's not inconvenient. It's natural, so don't fight it." He wrapped his arms around me. "Good night,

Gwyneth."

"Good night, Your Dallas." I snuggled deeper into his chest, smiling even as exhaustion overtook me.

I'd almost fallen asleep when he kissed my hair. "I love you, Gwyneth," he whispered.

Maybe he hadn't meant for me to hear, but I refused to pretend anymore. I clutched his chest. "I love you, too."

And then I blissfully fell asleep in his arms.

CHAPTER 13
UNDER A FALLING SKY

I WOKE UP AND HEARD DALLAS SPEAKING ANGRILY TO someone. "What do you mean, he *ordered* me to return?"

I sat up, blinking, and found myself alone in the big bed. Sunlight streamed through the windows.

"Your Highness, please." Mira Kinney's voice wafted from the adjacent suite. "The king said it was imperative that we return at once. I've already dispatched a separate crew to stay and film the West family at the ribbon-cutting ceremony this morning. Everything will go as we originally planned."

"No it will not. Miss West and I won't be here for the ceremony, and my meeting with the citizens of Four won't happen!"

Mira sighed. "The king said he had urgent business he needed you to attend to. He didn't elaborate."

"You bloody well know what he's doing. He's sabotaging this visit. He doesn't want me to speak the truth, and now he's yanking my leash and bringing me to heel."

Dallas went quiet, and I imagined him angrily pacing. "Did you send the footage back to the palace last night?"

"Yes, of course I did," Mira said. "Tariq and the production crew wanted to begin editing it as soon as possible. It's supposed to air tomorrow night."

"My father saw that tape, and he heard me talking about telling the truth. That's why we're heading back to the palace. He wants to censor me, and he wants no mention of rebel connections aired on national television."

My heart did a somersault, but not the fun kind. The painful, scared kind.

"Your Highness..." Mira sounded pleading.

"Don't you bloody 'Your Highness' me. I'll wake Gwyneth, and we'll be downstairs shortly. Please have the kitchen prepare a meal for her. And no cameras in the car on the ride home, Mira. I'm done performing tricks for the moment."

"Yes, Your Highness. I'm just not sure how to spin this for the audience at home."

"That's your problem, not mine. Do your job and figure it out. I'll see you shortly." I heard the door to the suite close, and a moment later, Dallas came into the bedroom, looking angry and distracted. He stopped when he saw me sitting up. "I guess you heard that."

"Are you all right?"

He raked a hand through his hair. "No, I'm not."

I patted the bed beside me. "Come here." He sank down, and I took his hand in mine. "The king has summoned you home?"

"Us." His voice was husky. "He's summoned us home."

"And you believe it was because he saw the tape of our conversation in the car? When you spoke of being honest about the rebels?"

"Yes." He stared at our entwined hands.

"What do you think he wants?"

He looked up at me, his face haunted. "He wants to shut me up."

I took a deep breath. "Maybe you should listen to him, Dallas."

"I've listened to him long enough." He sprang up and started pacing again. "I'm tired of his lies and how he manipulates everyone around him. Every inch of freedom he gives me, he takes away. He says he wants to raise me to rule, and yet he treats me like a child, unable to make decisions even for myself. I am *done* with him, Gwyneth."

"You can't be done with him. He's your father."

Dallas's eyes blazed. "He might be my father, but I no longer believe that he wants the best things for the settlements. No, he might be my father, but he is no longer my king."

"Bloody hell, don't say things like that!" I sat up, my nerves thrumming. "He'll accuse you of treason and throw you in the dungeons next to Balkyn!"

"That might not be the worst thing."

"Dallas, please. We've talked about this. The settlements need you. *I* need you. I understand you're angry, but you've got to calm down enough to have a rational conversation with him."

He clenched his fists and kept pacing. "He's going to

tell me I can't talk about the rebels, and he's going to tell me that I can't choose you because of your rebel connections."

I swallowed hard. I feared that was *exactly* what the king would say. "You still need to hear him out. He *is* the king, and he's also your father. You might not see it, but perhaps he really does have your best interests at heart."

He stopped and stared at me. "You think it's in our best interests to keep lying to our people about what we are and what they've lost?"

"No."

"Do you think it's in our best interests for my father to have me marry *Tamara*?"

"Maybe he'll ask you to consider one of the other girls." My voice came out small.

Dallas shook his head. "And you would let me go? You would stand by and watch me with someone else?"

I stood and went to him then wrapped my arms around his large, tense shoulders. "It would shatter my heart, Dallas. But if you believed it was the right thing, that it was best for your family and for the settlements, I would respect that."

"You want me to put my duty before my heart?" He sounded anguished.

"No, of course I don't. Because I'm a selfish cow, and I couldn't bear it." I laughed, trying to lighten the mood. "I'm trying to be supportive. But I'm not a royal—I've no idea of the sort of pressure you're under from your father. I'm saying that I support you and also that I don't want you to lose everything because of me. So hear your father out. Things will work out in the end, I know it."

He held me tightly. "How do you know?"

"Because you said they would, and you're the prince."

But as he held me, part of me worried he'd been wrong all along and that Mira had been right. The stars did not favor us.

And I did not know how to fight the stars.

❧

WE SAT IN SILENCE ON THE WAY BACK TO THE PALACE. I was sad that I didn't get to say goodbye to my family, but I didn't mention it. Dallas clearly had enough on his mind.

It didn't seem possible, but the competition would be over by week's end. Either I would be reunited with my family in celebration, or I'd be dropped on their doorstep, a sobbing mess. I took cold comfort from the fact that, either way, it wouldn't be long before I saw them again.

Dallas stared out the window, lost in his own thoughts. It was too bad we weren't taking advantage of the lack of cameras and snogging our brains out, but he seemed upset, with good reason.

"Will you go away again tonight, with Blake or Shaye?" I finally asked after a long silence.

He leaned against the seat. "I'm supposed to."

I waited for him to go on. When he didn't, I asked, "But?"

He shrugged. "*But* I'm just about done with this contest."

"You can't quit now. The whole country's watching. They're rooting for you, and it's only a few more days."

The muscle in his jaw jumped. "I'm not going to live a lie, Gwyneth."

I took a deep breath. "I'm not asking you to. I *am* asking you to be reasonable and to avoid burning a bridge with your father. Not because he is the king. Because he is your family."

"He isn't being reasonable, and he isn't listening. I think it's time to fight fire with fire."

"Dallas, please. Is my brother being reasonable? No, he is not. And yet, I love him still. I will continue to try to persuade him to listen to me, if not to see my side of the story. That's *my* duty, and I daresay it's yours, too. You can't just abandon your family. Not without trying first."

He blew out a deep breath. "Sometimes it feels as though I'm slamming my head into a wall, expecting the wall to just pick up and move out of my way."

"I understand." I thought of Balkyn, glaring at me with hate in his eyes. "No one said it would be easy. But think about the competition and everything that you've accomplished since it's begun. Finish what you started. Continue your good work of building a relationship with the settlers. Everything's changing. I could feel it when we were home and especially when we were at the center. People are excited. People have hope, which they haven't had for years. Don't undo the progress that you've made."

"Everyone was excited about the center. I'm very proud of it. The energy in Four was palpable." He was quiet, then he nodded. "You might be... Why, Gwyneth, you're right."

"I know I am!" Encouraged, I smiled. "So while I'm on a roll, I shall continue. You have to think long term, not short term. And here's another bit of wisdom. Do not cut off your nose merely to spite your face."

Dallas arched an eyebrow, the ghost of a smile appearing on his lips. "Have you been hanging out with Eve recently?" We often joked that Eve was the most philosophical person we knew.

"Of course I have." I reached for his hand. "It's nice to see you smile."

The smile vanished, replaced by a grimace. "I rather think it'll be in short supply when we get to the palace."

My stomach sank. I was nervous about what was waiting for us. The prince had more dates, there was the king's anger to deal with, my brother... Together, it all seemed like more than I was equipped to handle.

Still, I put my head on Dallas's shoulder. We would be separated upon our return, and I refused to waste another moment. "We have our happy bubble for now. And I'm so glad for it."

He gently stroked my hair. "As am I, Gwyneth. As am I."

CHAPTER 14
DEATH OF A THOUSAND CUTS

As was the custom, the palace's staff waited to greet us on the front stairs. They'd lined up neatly with expectant smiles on their faces. Tariq and the king waited near the door. My breath hitched as I saw them. Neither one of them was smiling.

Our driver parked the SUV, and the sentinel in the passenger seat opened his door.

"Wait," Dallas commanded. "Give us a moment. Let the camera crew set up, and then bring us out."

The sentinel nodded. "As you wish, Your Majesty."

Dallas hit the button for the privacy screen and turned to me, his eyes blazing. "I'm a bloody fool for not having you in my arms this entire time."

I reached out and stroked his face. "You're no fool. What we have is strong. You will take me in your arms again, I'm sure of it. We don't have to rush or act like every second we have together is our last."

He winced. "My father is ready to pounce. I need you

to promise me that you'll keep your head down and stay out of harm's way. If you're not at a lesson or a meal, please, stay in your chambers. It's best if my father doesn't even see you. I don't want you on his radar."

I nodded shakily. "I promise."

"And *I* promise to deal with him and to sort this out. You have my word that I will do everything to protect you, as well as Balkyn." He took my hands. "If I decide to continue with the Pageant—"

"Which *you must*—"

"—I won't see you for the next two days. Keep to yourself and do not speak of your brother. Trust no one, Gwyneth. I'll be thinking of you every moment."

He came closer and gently put his lips to mine. The kiss quickly turned into a deep, stormy embrace, our tongues tangling. I threw my arms around his neck, and he pulled me tightly against him, his hands running down my back, as if trying to memorize the planes of my body.

When he pulled away, I felt bereft, as if I might cry. He tapped me on the chin. "We're going to be okay."

"O-of course we are."

He took a deep breath and briefly closed his eyes. When he opened them, the storm had passed, and his gaze was clear. "I love you, Gwyneth. And I will fight for us."

"I love you, too." But I wanted to say more. *Do not fight so hard you lose yourself. Because of all the outcomes I can't bear to think about...*

"Are you ready?" he asked.

"Yes." *No.*

Dallas rapped on the privacy screen, and a moment later, the sentinel opened the door. Then we headed out, first into the sunshine and then into whatever darkness awaited us inside the palace.

"AH! WILL YOU LOOK WHAT THE CAT DRAGGED IN? You didn't last long, did you?" Tamara merrily sipped her sparkling water as I shuffled into the common room. "I daresay this competition's wrapped up!"

"Shut it, Tamara." I had no patience for her ribbing. I'd just seen the prince practically dragged off by his father, who'd been gesturing angrily when I saw them disappear down the hall. My stomach roiled, thinking about what the king had to say regarding our visit to Settlement 4.

I joined Tamara, Shaye, and Blake at their table, grabbing an apple from the fruit bowl. I listlessly turned it over. "Hi," Blake and Shaye said, both sounding tentative. I must have looked a mess.

"Hey."

Tamara tossed her raven waves over her shoulder and scrutinized me. "Ooh, someone's in a cranky mood. I'm sure it's difficult, watching what you want slip through your fingers." She held up her left hand and inspected it in the light. "Speaking of fingers, I can't wait to see what the royal engagement ring looks like, and I *really* can't wait to see it on me!"

"Didn't we just talk about this?" Blake scoffed.

"Decent Human Being Lesson Number One—Don't be a cow!"

Tamara shrugged. I noticed that her peach lip gloss precisely matched her gown, and for some reason, this enraged me. She waggled her perfectly groomed eyebrows at me. "I can't wait to see your tape, to see how badly you screwed up this time."

"Who said she screwed up?" Shaye frowned from across the table. Even with her dour expression, my friend looked lovely in a deep-rose dress, her hair in an artfully messy updo.

"Of course she screwed up! She got shipped home early. Everyone's talking about it." Tamara leaned forward, her eyes sparkling. "My maids said the king himself called off the date. He didn't want his son anywhere near her. I guess you're too much of an urchin, huh, Gwyn? Neither you nor your family are good enough for His Highness."

Something inside me snapped.

"Don't you ever talk about my family like that!" I grabbed Tamara's hair and yanked her head backward. She yelped, and I got in her face. "Say another word and it's bye-bye, bouncy waves. I'll rip them right out of your head."

"Gwyneth." Shaye leaned forward, looking nervous.

"I say go for it." Blake popped a bite of granola into her mouth. "She deserves it. And here I was, trying to give her Decent Human Being lessons."

Tamara tried to elbow me, but I caught her arm and squeezed. "Let me go, you lowlife!" She struggled against me and almost got free—all that working out had made her quite strong.

But adrenaline thrummed through me, helping me keep my grip. "Say you're sorry, at least for what you said about my family. I care very little what you think about me."

Her gaze turned steely. "I'm sorry." She didn't sound like she meant it, but as I really had no idea how to relieve her of her hair, I let her go.

She immediately jumped up. "You're going to pay for that, wench!"

"Oh, do sit down." Blake motioned to Tamara's empty seat. "Let's not turn this into any more of a circus —it's already close enough to being one, with just a few days left. Everyone needs to relax."

Tamara put her hands on her hips. "It's not *my* fault that she's coming unhinged."

"I'm not coming unhinged, you wanker."

Tamara opened her mouth as if to argue, but the common room door opened. Perhaps as a sign from the universe that I really should prepare myself for a crap day, Tariq sauntered in. He strolled to our table and inspected us slowly, one by one, his gaze finally coming to rest on Tamara. "What's going on? I heard yelling from down the hall."

Tamara pointed at me, her chest dramatically heaving. "She pulled my hair!"

Tariq's gaze found mine. A small smile hid under his mustache. "Gwyneth?"

I knew I should locate my game face, but it seemed

woefully out of reach. I scowled at him. "She insulted my family. And I didn't actually hurt her."

"Physically assaulting the other contestants is in direct violation of the competition's code of conduct," Tariq scolded. "I might have to take this up with the king."

"You'll do no such thing!" Blake slammed her spoon down on the table, making us all jump. "Tamara was being a cow to Gwyneth. She got what she deserved. Bullying is also against the code of conduct, I reckon, and Tamara's a textbook bully. Do you want me to report your little pet?"

Tariq cleared his throat, then smiled tightly at Blake. "That won't be necessary, my dear. I think we all need to take a step back. Tensions are running high this close to the end of the competition."

Tamara looked sour. "That doesn't make it okay for her to put her filthy urchin hands on me. She should be punished."

"Of course she should, my dear. But we'll all be punished for our wrongs in the end, so take some comfort from karma." He fluttered his eyelashes at her. "But for now, let's move on. I have several announcements." He cleared his throat, apparently waiting for us all to hang on his every word. "First things first, I'd like to congratulate Miss West on her visit home with the prince. I've watched the tape, and it's quite compelling. You did very well, Miss West."

Tamara narrowed her eyes at me. If she were a cat— or perhaps a snake—she would've hissed.

"Of course, your visit was cut short because His Majesty required the prince back at home. Such a pity." Tariq's eyes glittered, and I wondered exactly what the king had told him.

The royal emissary cleared his throat and continued. "Shaye, you have the next home visit. You're headed to Twenty-Four with the prince this morning. It's a long journey, so we want to send you off as soon as possible."

Shaye's cheeks heated with two hectic spots of color. "Of course."

Tamara arched an eyebrow at her. "I sure hope His Highness enjoys a nice mud hut and maybe a savory rat stew."

Blake jerked her thumb in Tamara's direction? "D'you see what I mean? She's a bully!"

Tariq frowned. "Tamara, please. Behave yourself. Sour grapes make you sound like a sore loser, not a front-runner."

She looked unsteadied by his negative remark but recovered quickly. "It's just that I've missed His Highness since we visited Eleven. We were so, so close—touching every second, stealing kisses every chance we got. Not seeing him for the past few days hurts terribly. Lovers aren't meant to be apart."

It took every ounce of my strength not to lunge at her. *Don't do it,* Blake mouthed.

Oh, but I longed to.

"Come. You have an etiquette lesson with Ms. Blakely, ladies." Tariq motioned for us to follow him.

"The cameras will join us for the rest of the morning. You might want to try to behave yourselves."

Blake tucked in next to me as we headed down the hall to one of the salons. "Don't let Tamara get to you. She's a drama queen. She'll stir up a hornet's nest and leave you to get stung."

I sighed. "I know you're right. I'm having a problem with impulse control today, I suppose. She doesn't usually get to me like this."

Blake shrugged. "It's the death of a thousand cuts."

"I'm sorry?"

"It means she nagged you bit by bit over the past few weeks. Now tensions are running high, and you're on the verge of snapping. It happens." She patted my back. "Don't worry about it."

"Uh... Thanks. How has the last day been?"

Blake yawned. "A bit boring, actually. Obviously I'm crap at giving lessons on how to be a decent human being. And I had my walk with the queen, which was basically a disaster. She barely said two words to me. Ooh, but the prince's brother is supposed to be coming to town. It's all my maids have been talking about."

"Austin? Do you know when he'll be here?"

"No, but I suspect we'll know as soon as he arrives. The rumor mill's fired up these days. Everyone's on edge because of the end of the competition."

We came even with Shaye, who was closely watching Tariq and Tamara ahead of us, whispering to each other. "Those two are up to something."

"Aren't they always?" Blake asked. "Two peas in a pod, they are."

I turned to Shaye. "Are you excited to go home and see your family?"

"Yes, absolutely. I can't wait. I'm nervous about what the prince will think of my hometown, of course. It *is* a bit muddy. But we don't eat rat stew." She jutted her chin. "At least, not with company."

"Don't let Tamara get to you," I scolded. "The prince is hardly a snob. He doesn't care what your house looks like or what's in your cupboards. He cares about the people in your settlement and what he can do to help them."

Shaye relaxed a little. "Is that what you learned during your visit?"

"Yes. He was very generous with Four. He started a community center there, with a medical clinic and a place for people to go back to school. It's quite magnificent, really."

"Do you think he'll do that in my district?"

I took Shaye's arm. "He wants to do them in every settlement. The center in Four had only been open for a few days, but there was so much activity there. They were already helping people."

"It would be wonderful if we could have one. Our people have been hurting since the war." Shaye looked hopeful.

"He'll do it. I know he will."

Tariq delivered us to the salon and nodded at Shaye. "It's time, Miss Iman. I'll escort you to your chambers."

Shaye smiled at us nervously. "Carry on, then."

"Good luck." I squeezed her hand.

"Have fun." Blake winked at her.

"Don't choke on a rat bone." Tamara tossed her hair and turned on her heel without another word.

"I might pack some stew in a thermos for her." Shaye narrowed her eyes. "A little souvenir might be just what she needs."

"Yes! I've been waiting for this." Blake held out her hand for a high five.

"Waiting for what?" Bewildered, Shaye slapped her hand.

"For you to get pissy about something. You're so good all the time." Blake reached down and hugged her. "It's nice to see you're human—although still better than the rest of us."

I hugged Shaye when Blake released her; I was going to miss my friend. "You *are* better than the rest of us. Have a good trip. Safe travels."

When I released her, Shaye's eyes shone with unshed tears. "Stop it, you two! I'm already upset about having to say goodbye to you at the end of the week."

"Don't think about it." Blake winked at her. "Unless you want to think about saying goodbye to Tamara, then by all means, proceed. Or better yet, pack her a savory rat stew. I agree, it might be just what she needs."

CHAPTER 15

THE PRINCE FROM THE NORTH

I KEPT DIGGING MY NAILS INTO MY PALMS SO I wouldn't fall asleep. The cameras were right next to us, and I couldn't very well get caught snoring on film. I was already in enough trouble.

Still, I struggled to pay attention. "It's imperative that you accept the serving dish from the left. Keep your hands in your lap, if that helps you. The point is, do not interrupt the flow of the dinner service. The dining room maids will have a fit." Ms. Blakely droned on and on, and I desperately wished I were back in the hotel bed with Dallas. *That* wouldn't be boring...

We were interrupted by a knock on the door. Tariq poked his head inside. "I'm so sorry to interrupt. However, His Royal Highness Austin Black has a break in his schedule. He'd like to meet the contestants."

"Of course!" Ms. Blakely looked excited for us. "Go ahead, ladies. Class dismissed."

Camera crew in tow, we quickly followed Tariq down

the hall. Burning with curiosity to meet Dallas's younger brother, I found that my pace almost outstripped the royal emissary's. "Where are we meeting him?" I asked, a bit breathlessly.

"In the gardens. His Highness has requested to inspect each of you out in the sunlight."

"Inspect us? Why?" Tamara asked, looking perplexed.

"He said he wants to get a good look at the 'crazy human girls'—his words, not mine—who would marry his brother." Tariq coughed. "His Highness has his own way of doing things, as you'll see shortly."

"Yay?" Blake said as we followed him outside to the courtyard.

The three of us stopped dead in our tracks when we saw the man who must have been the younger prince. He was in the center of the courtyard, shirtless, performing combat training with a sentinel. His large muscles rippled, the sun glinting off his pale skin, as he went on the attack.

"*Yay.*" Blake fanned herself.

Austin and the sentinel were sparring, each wielding a long stick exactly like the one I'd seen Eve practice with. The prince twirled his stick, then lunged at the sentinel. Their weapons cracked together fiercely. Sweat poured down Austin's chiseled physique. Like Dallas, he was tall and strapping; his skin glistened in the sunlight. But Austin was slightly shorter than his brother and perhaps more powerfully built. I cursed myself for not seeing Dallas's chest while I had the chance, back in our hotel room. Then I would've been able to properly compare them....

Tamara wrinkled her nose. "Seems a bit rabid, doesn't he?"

"Maybe a bit. Hmm, today's gotten more interesting." Blake seemed positively cheerful. "I do love a good fight."

Austin grunted and ducked as the soldier swung at his head. Crouching on the ground, Austin surprised the guard by suddenly pressing his weapon into his chest, heart center. "Gotcha."

The sentinel cursed and threw down his stick.

"You have to anticipate this move, Timmy. It's your undoing when you think you have the upper hand. I would've skewered you if this were a real fight." Austin got up, wiped his hands on his trousers, and shook his opponent's hand. "You'll get me one of these days."

"You've been saying that for years." The soldier laughed.

Austin turned and caught sight of us staring. "Looks like we've got an audience." He held out his hand, and another nearby guard handed him his shirt.

He pulled it on, his muscles rippling, and Blake groaned. She leaned closer and whispered, "Make him take it back off. That's a bloody crime against nature!"

The younger prince strode toward us, and although his physique and coloring were similar, his eyes were different from Dallas's. My prince had dark-brown eyes. Austin's were a brilliant, unusual mixture of amber and hazel. His gaze raked over each of us. "You're a crazy lot, aren't you? Or desperate."

Frowning, Tariq bowed. "Your Highness. These are three of the remaining contestants. The fourth has just left with your brother for Settlement Twenty-Four."

Austin frowned back at Tariq. "Yes, yes, I know. My brother and his motorcade and press secretary have fled. Can't say I blame him."

Tariq cleared his throat. "Moving right along, let me introduce you. This is Miss Gwyneth West from Settlement Four, Miss Blake Kensington from Settlement Fifteen, and Miss Tamara Layne from Settlement Eleven. Ladies, please allow me to introduce you to His Royal Highness, Prince Austin Black, Crown Prince of the United Settlements."

We curtsied as Austin glared at the royal emissary. "I'm not the crown prince of the settlements, you bloody whinger. I'm the prince of the North."

Tariq fake-smiled so hard I thought his face might break. "Of course, Your Highness."

Austin jerked his chin at him. "Leave us. I'll get to know these ladies without you sniveling about."

A dark shadow passed over Tariq's face, but as soon as he could control himself, it passed. "Yes, Your Majesty. The cameras will have to keep filming, though."

Austin snorted. "Let 'em. I'll quite enjoy it."

Tariq looked as though he might be having second thoughts about leaving the cameras with the outspoken younger prince. But as he was clearly outranked, he stalked off without another word.

"Now that I can breathe without smelling His Cloyingness, let's get to know each other, shall we?" He stepped forward and bowed. "I'm Austin, Dallas's younger brother. I've been called down here so that I can watch one of you loons get engaged to my brother. Come. The servants have set out some tea for you. Let's see what's going on inside your heads."

Blake looked excited, Tamara looked suspicious, and I reminded myself to be careful as we followed Austin through a path in the garden to a large table set with tea, biscuits, and a bottle of red wine. "Would anyone care for something stronger?" the prince asked as the servers poured our tea.

We all politely declined.

The three of us sat, surrounded by servants, the film crew, and the rose bushes. Austin stalked around the table, inspecting each of us. "I've watched all the episodes. I know each one of you."

Tamara sniffed prettily, as though she were trying to subtly marginalize the prince while simultaneously flirting with him. "Oh, really? And what is it you think you know?"

"You," he said, pointing at Tamara. "You're the snobby rich one. The one who's always eye-snogging the cameras."

Tamara cleared her throat primly, even as she instinctively stuck her chest out. "I beg your pardon."

"Oh, I can tell, just by looking at you, that you don't need *my* pardon. Just keep sipping your tea with your pinky out, wearing your fancy clothes, and you'll land on your feet."

Tamara frowned at her hand. Her pinky was indeed extended.

"And you. You're the one my brother hasn't kissed." Austin came closer to Blake and looked her up and down. Blake's thick, long blond hair tumbled around the shoulders of her pale-yellow gown.

She chuckled, her pretty face lighting up with good humor. "Yeah, that's my claim to fame."

"What's his bloody problem?" Austin shook his head, as if this did not compute. "Stand up for a minute if you would, my lady."

Without a second thought, Blake raised herself to her considerable height. Austin stalked closer toward her. They were each six feet tall, their eyes meeting at the same level. "Are you checking to see if you're taller than me?" Blake frowned.

"I just wanted to see it for myself." Austin considered her. "Dallas mentioned you were quite tall."

"He's a genius, that brother of yours."

The younger prince chuckled. "Thank you for indulging me, my lady. I haven't been around many human women. And I've never seen one as tall as me."

"So not only am I the one that your brother's never kissed, I'm also the tallest." Blake plopped down in her chair a bit glumly. "I'm so happy to entertain you."

Austin tilted his chin, his gaze never leaving hers. "I also heard you're quite good at basketball."

Blake preened a bit, buoyed by the compliment. "Yes, I am. Quite."

"Maybe we can play together." Austin smiled at her,

and she smiled back while the rest of us just sat there, a bit uncomfortably.

The younger prince eventually stopped staring at Blake and turned to me. "And finally, there's Miss West. You're the one who's causing all the ruckus."

"I... I am?" I pretended not to know what he was talking about.

"You're a terrible liar. I've seen it for myself on your tapes."

"Oh?" I tried to be nonchalant as I stirred my tea.

"You. In my office." He jerked his thumb toward a path through the roses.

"You have an office?"

"It's an expression. Come with me, please. No cameras." The look he gave the production crew stopped them dead in their tracks. "Film these two. They're better looking than me, anyway." He winked at Blake, and she blushed.

I hadn't known Blake *could* blush. I raised my eyebrow at her while following Austin, but she demurely added another sugar cube to her tea and ignored me.

We left them as Austin led me down a path. We veered to the left and ended up in a pretty little private garden. Large Asters bloomed in yellow, pink, and orange. He motioned at a stone bench; I took this as an order to sit, which I obeyed. Much like his brother, Austin had an air about him, as if he expected me to do exactly as he wished. I supposed that was a by-product of being raised as both a prince and a vampire.

"So." He put his hands on his hips and surveyed me. "Are you getting on all right without my brother?"

"He just left an hour ago. I think I'll make it."

He wrinkled his nose. "The way he made it sound, I thought you'd be boo-hooing by now. *He* probably is, in the backseat of his fancy car. That poor other girl won't even know what hit her."

I chuckled. "I assure you, Dallas won't be boo-hooing. He'll be the perfect gentleman, as always."

"Is that what you call it when he snogs your face off? He's being a perfect gentleman then?" Austin's eyes sparkled merrily.

I cleared my throat. "What is it you wanted to talk to me about?"

"Are you serious about my brother?"

"Serious how?"

He leveled his gaze at me. "Don't play with me, Miss West. I want to know if you're serious about becoming his wife."

"I am." The words tasted funny coming out of my mouth. I hadn't bald-faced admitted this to anyone else.

"And for what reason, may I ask?"

"Because I'm in love with him." I blurted the words out before I could stop myself.

Austin chuckled and raked a hand through his closely cropped hair. The gesture was so similar to one by Dallas, I couldn't help staring. "So it's true, then."

"What's true?"

"You really are a madwoman. What sort of a human marries a beast like my brother?"

I shot to my feet. "Pardon me, but Dallas is no beast! He's the kindest, most gallant, most—"

Austin waved me off. "Blah, blah, blah. You don't need to sing his praises to me. I love him, too. But that doesn't mean I think this is a good idea. Quite the opposite."

"What do you mean?" I sank down onto the bench, my heart thudding. "Why do you think it's a bad idea?"

Austin grimaced. "Because it was my father's, and that's usually a telltale sign."

"It's certainly not your father's idea that Dallas marry *me*, if that makes you rest easier."

"I heard that. You come from a family of rebels?"

I sighed. "Something like that." I wanted to tell him the whole story, but I didn't dare.

"I see. But despite my father's objections, I know full well that my brother will do as he pleases. And from what he's told me, you're what pleases him."

I smiled a little, my cheeks heating. "Thank you for that."

"But there's more than one problem with all this. It's not just my father's historically bad judgment."

"Go on."

Austin crossed his arms against his powerful chest. "My family has no business mixing with humans."

"You looked like you wanted to mix with Blake pretty badly back there," I quipped.

Austin laughed. "You caught that, eh? Well, she's... refreshing. There's something about her."

"Yeah, like the fact that she's tall and gorgeous." *And probably smells delicious to you.*

"She's fetching all right, but this isn't about your friend. Back to you and my brother. Vampires have no business marrying humans. It's not what we do."

"Then why does your father want your brother to do it?"

Austin scrubbed a hand over his face. "Because he's lost his home, and it's made him lose his mind."

"Explain. *Please*. Dallas won't get into the specifics of what happened up north. I don't know why your family had to leave your lands to come here."

"They didn't have to leave, but my father's always been too ambitious. After the blight hit, there wasn't enough left up north for him to stay interested in sticking around."

"What blight?"

"The one that ruined our lands and turned everything dark. Mind you, vampires like the dark, but even this was too much for most of us."

"I still don't understand."

He sighed. "A blight's like a virus. But the land is its host, not a person. Our lands got sick. A lot of things died—except the bloody werewolves and a particularly nasty breed of gnomes. The virus left the worst of us to rot with each other."

"What are the werewolves and gnomes like, exactly? Do they fight against you? Do they drink human blood, too?"

"No, they don't drink human blood! Are you daft?"

I threw up my hands. "No one will tell me about

these creatures. I didn't even know they existed until recently!"

"There's all manner of things up north. But don't bother yourself with creatures you don't need to understand. Honestly, the less you know, the safer you are." Austin eyed me. "In any event, my father wasn't interested in ruling a bunch of bloody gnomes while fighting off the werewolves. There were lots of volunteers to leave the North in its decrepit state. That's how he assembled such a large army. He'd had the settlements in his sights for a long time. The blight gave him a sense of urgency about it."

"But why did you stay up north? It sounds terrible."

"I wouldn't ever leave my home. I will fight for it until the day I die." Austin leveled his gaze to meet mine. "And I'd never come down here to rule a bunch of wanking *humans*. I think Dallas and my father are mad. Vampires have a symbiotic relationship with your kind, and it's not exactly loving. It's like your relationship with livestock—keep 'em in a pen until you put 'em on a plate."

I swallowed hard. "Dallas only drinks donated blood."

"Oh does he, now? Such a hero, my brother." He took a step closer. "Don't let him fool you. We had slaves up north, you should know. He drank from them just like the rest of us."

I raised my chin. "And where are these slaves now?"

Austin sighed. "I only have a few left. I'm hoping to bring some volunteers back with me."

"You won't do any such thing!" I shot to my feet

again. "If the staff wants to donate blood for you, fine. But you won't be taking *slaves* back north with you. Slaves don't exist in the settlements, and I won't stand for you continuing such a barbaric tradition."

He started laughing, deep from his belly. He shook his head. "You telling me what to do—in some ways, Gwyneth, you'd fit right in."

"I suppose I did cross a line there. It's just that I don't want to see you do something terrible to our people. I believe we can move past all that and have a brighter future. One in which you don't have us on an...er...plate."

"My mother was right about you."

I looked up sharply. "Right how?"

"She said you were ridiculously optimistic, just like him."

"I beg your pardon?"

Austin sat back on his heels, regarding me. "Both you and my brother think that love will save the day, and that humans and vampires can coexist. In fact, you think you're going to skip off merrily into the sunset together, hand in hand, happily ever after. I say that's hogwash. *I* say, you make my brother vulnerable. The best thing you could do is to walk away from him."

My heart twisted. I'd quite expected to like Austin, but I felt as if he were turning my already chaotic world further upside down. "Why would you say such a thing?"

His face softened. "Because someone has to. And if you truly love my brother, you'll listen."

CHAPTER 16
THE GREAT DIVIDE

"I CAN TELL I'VE UPSET YOU. MY BROTHER WILL HAVE my head on a spike." Austin looked up at the sky, as if searching for instructions on what to do next.

"I want to hear what you have to say." My limbs felt heavy as I sank down onto the cold stone bench. Even though the sun shone brightly, I was chilled to the bone. "I have some of my own concerns, anyway."

His eyes glittered. "As well you should. If you didn't have any reservations about marrying into this family, I'd say you need to be committed."

"Because you are vampires or because you are royals?" I asked.

"Because both. And therein lies the problem." Austin stalked the tiny garden, clearly trying to align his thoughts.

"You said I'd made your brother vulnerable. Please explain."

He nodded. "Our enemies here are the human rebels.

To date, they've been unable to succeed in their efforts against us. That's because a human can rarely, if ever, kill a vampire. Our distinct advantage is their undoing, and they're too stupid to figure out that it's never going to get better. They keep trying to take back their lands."

I coughed. "Perhaps they're too ridiculously optimistic." I still smarted from the queen's description of me.

"Are all of you like that?" Austin asked, genuinely curious. "That hopeful?"

"Maybe, to a point. I think the human condition might be to believe that, eventually, things will work out the way you want them to. Or at least, to hope they will." But then I remembered the hollow look in Balkyn's eyes, the hate that burned just below the surface of his skin, too hot to touch. "But not all of us are like that."

"But *you* are. You think that you and my brother can bring change to the settlements and have united peace here. A real future. Dallas told me that himself. He sees you as partners, ruling the nation together, human and vampire."

I raised my eyebrows. "I'm sure your father won't let that happen."

"Not if he gets his way. But if anyone can give him a run for his money, it's my big brother. They're both pigheaded, another reason I like staying up north just fine, thank you very much. I've been doused one too many times getting in the middle of their pissing contests. But anyway, back to the point—you, being bad for my brother."

I frowned. "Go on."

"The reason you make him vulnerable is simple. You can die. The rebels can't ever get to him or my father, but they sure as hell can get to you. You're fragile, weak. If the rebels don't kill you, childbirth can, or the plague, or any of the other hundred things that humans are susceptible to. You're flimsy, Gwyneth. You have a short, perilous shelf life."

"I would consider being turned, but I don't think Dallas would hear of it."

"Of course he wouldn't." Austin grunted. "He's a bloody purist! He thinks you're perfect just the way you are. His bleeding, optimistic heart wouldn't dream of sinking his fangs into you, even as he craves your blood. He doesn't believe in changing humans, never has. He thinks we're born the way we're supposed to be and that we should accept our lot in life."

"He is rather reasonable in that way. He won't play God."

"And yet you have him on a pedestal and worship him as though he were. Enough. It would take a lifetime to debate whether turning others is ethical, just as we could go round and round about the morality of our respective dietary choices. My point is, I don't see that you're worth all the fuss."

"Well." My cheeks heated. "Tell me how you really feel, Austin."

He tilted his chin. "It's not because I don't like you— I do, very much so. Like I told you, I've watched every episode of this contest. If I had to choose one of you crazy humans for my brother, I would choose you. You're perfect for him. You calm him down even as you inspire him, and I believe since he's been with you, he's seeing things more clearly. You're his emotional eyeglasses, if you will."

"I'm sorry?"

"You help him see better. Father's tried to keep him in the dark about the true state of the settlements because he knows my brother won't tolerate injustice. Where my father is slow to make change, Dallas is bold. He's not afraid to try new things, but my father's very set in his ways. That dynamic's always been difficult between them, but now that Dallas has come of age, and he will marry soon, his point of view has become more of a threat to my father. You exacerbate that. You've helped him see what's really going on, and it's changed him. For the better."

"So why are you saying I'm bad for him? I don't understand."

Austin resumed pacing. "My brother loves you—that's the problem. Loving you makes him vulnerable. He will fight my father in order to be with you. It could fracture our family. And that's only one area where you expose him to weakness."

A dull headache formed in between my eyes. "What else? How else do I weaken him?"

"Your life, in comparison to his, will be insignificant. And yet you'll make him vulnerable, as a leader *and* as a man. The rebels could take you and kill you, or worse. That will cause another great war. So if you marry him, he's either fighting my father or the rebels to protect you. Enemies at every turn, the way I see it."

My head throbbed. "Are you quite done?"

"Not yet. Because even if that doesn't happen—if he doesn't have to rise up against our father, if he doesn't have to bleed thousands of rebels in order to reclaim you —he'll still lose you. You are human, and he is vampire. Your life passes so quickly. You will widow him while he's still young. Why would you choose to put him through that? What's the point?"

My mouth went dry. "He said that...he said that we could have a life together, a child. And I'm still young. The years ahead of me might be insignificant to you, but I could live to be quite old, for a human."

"For a *human*," Austin echoed. "This is what I mean. Our kinds mixing is madness. No good will come of it. I know my brother wants to marry you, but you will only bring him heartache."

I couldn't get any words out. I stared straight ahead.

Austin sighed and held out his hand. "Come. Let me return you to your friends. I am sorry to speak so harshly, but you've been living in a bubble with my brother. You don't know enough to understand how easy it is to burst happiness like that. It's not built to last, I'm afraid."

I wearily accepted his hand and followed him in silence down the path. "Austin, I should thank you. You've given me much to think about, even if it makes me unhappy."

He nodded, stopping for a moment before we reached the others. "I could tell from the tapes I watched that you truly have feelings for Dallas and he for you. So even if he married one of these other girls, it would be better for him."

"Why?" It felt as though my heart were drying out and starting to crack.

"Because he doesn't love them. He loves you. Love makes you vulnerable, Gwyneth. And a king has no business being vulnerable."

* * *

I DRAGGED MYSELF THROUGH THE REST OF THE DAY—another lesson from Ms. Blakely, followed by dinner—and retreated early to my room. I couldn't get Austin's words out of my head, and I didn't know what to do.

I heard a knock on the door. "Who is it?"

"It's me, and I have chocolate!" Blake called. "Open the door."

I groaned and let her in. "What's going on?"

"That's what I'm bloody well here to ask you!" She flopped into a chair and put a tray heaped with brownies and cupcakes on the coffee table. "I brought emergency supplies from the kitchen. So tell me, what was with the moping all afternoon? You barely said a word, and you were white as a ghost."

"I don't want to talk about it," I mumbled.

"Here." Blake placed a chocolate cupcake on a napkin and shoved it into my hands. "It has cream cheese frosting, and it tastes like angels made it. So eat up, and then you better tell me what's going on. Tariq told me I'm leaving with the prince as soon as he gets back from Shaye's. I can't go unless I know you're okay."

"I am not okay. But you're right—this tastes divine." I devoured the cupcake.

"Tell me what's bothering you." Blake's pretty face twisted with worry. "What did Austin say to make you so upset?"

"Speaking of Austin, did I see you *blush* earlier today? You two were eye-snogging each other, and then he winked at you, and then you blushed. That was certainly unexpected!" I hadn't dared to ask her anything in front of Tamara, but I'd been dying to know what she thought of the younger prince.

"He's very...manly, isn't he? Even though he's a vampire." Blake cleared her throat. "I couldn't look at him without turning red. I don't know what that's about. It's never happened to me before."

"Well, I do. It means you have a crush on the prince's younger brother, when you're supposed to have a crush on the prince."

"Yeah, well." Blake shrugged and grabbed a giant brownie. "You can't fight biology, I guess. Sometimes the crush chooses *you*. You of all people should know that."

"What's that supposed to mean?"

"It means you would probably never have chosen to love the prince, but here you are, in love with him."

I shook my head. "I don't think I should be, though."

"What do you mean?"

"That's what Austin and I were talking about. I don't

want to trouble you with the specifics." I started tearing my napkin into tiny pieces.

"Will you stop talking like that?"

"Like what?"

Blake snorted. "Like talking about your feelings is a burden to me. I might still be a contestant, but I'm not your competition, Gwyn. I consider you my friend, you know. I was sort of hoping you felt the same way."

"Of course you're my friend, and of course I feel the same way." I sighed. "Part of the reason I don't want to share details with you is because I want to protect you. Can you understand that?"

"Not without more details." Blake grinned.

"Oh, fine. Here's a start. I have family connections to the rebels."

"So does Shaye," Blake said through a mouthful of brownie. "So did half the girls here."

"I know. But the king objects to me because of it, and so...that's that. And Austin objects to me because he thinks I make Dallas vulnerable."

"How so?"

"Because I'm human, and that makes me weak. Austin doesn't believe in humans and vampires mixing."

"What?" Blake's face fell. "I thought he liked me."

"He definitely likes you—he told me so."

Her blue eyes grew huge. "What did he say? Tell me everything!"

"He said you were refreshing, and..." I tried to remember his exact words. "Fetching. Yes, he said you were fetching."

"But he thinks humans are below them, somehow?" Blake wrinkled her nose. "I'm pretty pissed my hormones decided to crush out on a bloke who's a racist."

"I don't know if he's a racist. He's more of a separatist."

"Same thing." She eyed the dessert tray again longingly. "I wish I weren't so stuffed. This is a bit depressing."

"I think he hasn't been around humans much before, so he doesn't understand that we can really get along. I mean, look at Eve and me. She's a vampire, and she's one of my best friends. We will always be friends, and our races don't matter. In fact, our differences are sort of fun. I like learning about vampires. I feel the same way about Dallas. It's exciting being with someone from a different background."

"But you would love him even if he were human. I know you would."

"Of course I would." I nodded. "I love him for who he is."

"This is the first time you've admitted it to me, you know. That you love him."

"You knew, anyway."

"Yes, I did." Blake smiled at me. "So why are you letting his separatist, prat little brother try to talk you out of it?"

"Because there's truth to what he said. I do make Dallas vulnerable. The rebels can hurt me in ways they can't hurt him—and then they can hurt him by hurting me. On top of that, I'll grow old. I'll die. In the end,

Dallas won't have that much time with me. It makes me wonder if all the trouble's worth the risk."

"Love is always a risk. It always makes you 'weaker,' if you want to look at it the way wanking Austin looks at it."

"I thought you liked him."

Blake grabbed one of the cupcakes. "I suppose I just liked his massive, heavily muscled chest. I can unlike that." She had a large helping of cream cheese frosting. "Loving anyone makes you more vulnerable. Even our families."

I winced, thinking of my brother. "You're right."

"I know I am. But that vulnerability doesn't mean you should hide from love. Otherwise, what's the point of getting out of bed in the morning?" She shook her head. "I've half a mind to lay into that Austin. He's really on my bad side, and I barely know him."

"Are you sure you're not just looking for an excuse to talk to him?"

She punched me lightly on the shoulder. "Don't be ridiculous, and don't listen to him."

But I have to. I opened my mouth then closed it, struggling to find the words to express how I felt.

"Cough it up, then." Blake nodded.

"I told you that I love Dallas, but I didn't tell you how much." My eyes pricked with tears, and I groaned. "He means everything to me, Blake. I would do anything to protect him. There's so many things against us—his father, the fact that I'm related to rebels, what his brother just said... It almost makes me feel as though I'm crazy not to stop and listen to all the warning bells going off. Literally everyone and everything is stacked against us. There was something Mira said, too, that the stars don't favor us."

"That sounds like vampire voodoo." She wrinkled her nose. "I don't believe that any of those reasons should keep you apart. If you love each other, you should be together. You should try."

"I'm worried that I'm the wrong choice for him. And all I want is what's right for him."

"You should let him have some say in this, I should think."

I sighed. "He won't listen to me, not about this."

"That's because you aren't being reasonable."

"No, I don't think that's true. To be reasonable, I have to consider the facts. Everyone who loves him has expressed their displeasure with me. His father made him leave during our visit to Four, and his brother basically told me I'd ruin Dallas's life if I accepted a proposal." I sank lower into my seat as the weight of the truth crashed around me: his family was against this. They were against *me*. The people who loved him best and had known him longest believed I was the wrong choice for him.

Who was I to argue with that?

"I think you're listening to the wrong people." Blake frowned.

"I'm listening to myself, Blake. They're telling me what I already thought, that my love puts Dallas at risk." I couldn't even begin to tell her the whole truth—about my brother in the dungeon, who'd tried to kill the prince, about how I'd let Benjamin Vale escape and he'd taken the lives of three guards.

Who had I been kidding? I'd let my love blind me, but what Austin said underlined the truth I already knew, deep in my belly. *It's not built to last, I'm afraid.*

"I think we should probably get going to bed." I smiled at Blake, trying to hide the fact that I was suddenly shaking. I needed to be alone.

She hugged me hard before she left. "Don't talk yourself in circles. Get some rest."

I didn't cry until she left the room. And she didn't need to know there were no more circles to talk myself into. What I'd said to Blake was the truth: my love made Dallas vulnerable. Everyone who loved him was against him choosing me.

The end was coming. I'd promised myself that I'd do what was best for him.

My decision had been made.

I was going to have to let him go.

"WHY AREN'T WE SEEING THE OTHER HOME-VISIT episodes?" Tamara's voice veered between wheedling and annoyance. The episodes had been shown to the settlement audience all week, but we hadn't been allowed to view them.

"We think it's best for the contestants to spend the rest of their time at the castle sequestered so that the grand finale comes as a real surprise. The final episode will be *ah*-mazing." Tariq nodded to her. "No one saw the final cut of your home visit, my dear, not even you. The other girls won't see theirs either. There are no unfair advantages."

"But I want to know why Gwyn had to come home early. I want to see how Mira spun it. And I want to know if Shaye does in fact live in a mud hut." She put her hands on her hips and pouted.

"And you will know. Once the contest is over, each contestant will get an authentic royal first edition of the entire series. You'll own it forever and can look back on all the fun whenever you wish."

Not at all placated by the offer, Tamara frowned. "That's not going to help me right now. I want to know what the audience knows. I want to know who the front-runner is."

"You know you crushed your home visit. Even Mira said so." Tariq beamed at her. "We just want you to relax and enjoy the rest of the competition, your final date and the finale, when His Highness announces his choice."

"I *am* looking forward to it." Somewhat soothed, she smiled back. "At least I have my walk with the queen this morning. Too bad His Highness has to go home with that big blond oaf and can't join us."

"I beg your pardon. I can hear you, you know! Did you learn nothing from our Basic Human Decency lessons?" Blake arched an eyebrow. "The big blond oaf can kick your arse, I'll remind you. So zip it, Your Haughtiness."

"I'm looking forward to kicking *you* out of the palace when I'm chosen as princess." Tamara smiled at Blake merrily. "I shall quite enjoy cleaning out all the riffraff."

"I'm sure Gwyn will enjoy having you thrown out on the front lawn when *she's* chosen." Blake grinned right back. "And I'll be in the front row, cheering."

"Gwyneth's not getting that proposal." Tamara clenched her hands into fists. "I'll run her out of the palace myself."

"Honestly, Tamara, shut it." My voice was hoarse from crying all night, but I'd told them I wasn't feeling well. "If the prince gives you the ring, I'll congratulate you, and then I'll show myself out."

Tamara turned her frown on me. "Will you go back to bed, already? No one wants your germs! You look chalky green, and chalky green is not my color. Plus, you're no fun when you don't fight back. You're almost as boring as Shaye."

"Keep talking like that about Shaye. She'll bring you rat stew, she will." Blake rubbed her hands together. "And I'll hold you down with my big oaf arms while she pours it down your throat."

"Honestly!" Tamara wrinkled her nose as if she smelled something putrid. "I don't know how you two beasts got chosen as finalists. You'd think the prince would have better taste. My word, I almost feel like I need to take a shower after sitting at the same table as you."

"Go on, then. Off you go. No one's stopping you." Blake took a bite of apple.

"Oh, fine. Enjoy your trip with His Highness. Don't do anything I wouldn't."

"That's a bloody short list," Blake said through a mouthful of food.

"And *please*, keep up that sort of behavior. You look like a supermodel, but you eat like a Neanderthal. You're doing us all a favor." Tamara tossed her hair indignantly then pointed a finger at me. "And you—I mean it—go to bed. Come back when you have some color in your cheeks and can fight. We've got to keep the momentum going. The audience is counting on us to keep things

lively if not"—she eyed Blake chomping on her apple
—"civilized."

She hustled off. "I'm going for my walk with Her
Majesty now. At least *she's* got some manners."

"Just don't piss her off like Eve did!" Blake called.

Tariq narrowed his eyes at her. "Please behave during
your home visit. The entire episode is about you." He
looked apprehensive at the thought.

"I can handle myself."

Tariq bowed. "Then please do so. The prince will
return shortly, then it will be time to go." He turned to
me. "Do you need a doctor?"

I shook my head. "No. It's just a cold."

"Back to bed with you, then. I'll dismiss you from
lessons for the rest of the day. But your final date with
the prince is tomorrow, as is Tamara's. I need you in top
form by then."

"Yes, Your Royal Emissary."

"Blake," Tariq continued, "you and Shaye will have
your dates after that. Then it's the finale, ladies."

I cleared my throat. "Will we all be going home,
immediately after the winner's announced?"

Blake looked at me sharply as Tariq nodded. "Yes,
arrangements will be made to escort the departing
contestants as soon as filming's complete. It's easier on
everyone that way."

I nodded. It would be better to be gone quickly.

"This whole competition's worked out better than I
ever dared hope." He rubbed his hands together. "The
atmosphere in the settlements is electric. It's all anyone's

talking about. It's going to be a celebration unlike any other, and then we have the royal wedding to plan, which will be the event of the century." He prattled on, but I swiftly tuned him out. The last thing I wanted to hear about was the royal wedding.

Finally, Blake and I were dismissed—me to my room, her to pack for her home visit.

"What's the matter with you?" she whispered.

I shrugged. "I'm not feeling well."

"Because you're actually sick or because you're making yourself sick?"

"Does it matter?" I pulled her in for a hug. "Have fun on your visit, and have a lovely time with your family."

"I will. I'll come see you as soon as I get back, okay?"

"Yes." I released her and swiftly headed to my chambers before I erupted into a fresh round of tears.

I'd just climbed under my blankets when I heard a knock on my door. *Bloody hell.* "Yes?" I croaked, hoping I sounded sicker than I felt so whoever it was would go away.

"May I come in?"

I sat up straight. "Eve?" She'd never come to my room before.

My friend came in and quickly closed the door behind her. She wore a dark tunic and trousers, her blond curls tracing her jawline. "Blake said you were hiding up here." She paced the length of the floor, nervous energy radiating off her.

"Eve? What's the matter?"

"We've got a problem, I'm afraid."

My stomach dropped. "What's wrong?"

Her blazing aqua eyes focused on me. "Wait, why're you in bed?"

"I'm sick." I blew my nose for effect.

"Why do you look like you've been up all night crying?"

"Because I've been up all night, crying. Now tell me what the problem is!"

She blew out a deep breath. "I did something, and someone found out about it. And it's not good."

"You're going to have to be a bit more specific."

She went to the window and stared out at the grounds. "I've been visiting your brother the past few days."

"How is he?"

She shook her head. "He's not doing well. And we have another problem, I'm afraid."

A frozen calm, laced with dread, descended over me. "What is it?"

"The queen's been sneaking about, following me." Eve turned to face me. "She knows who Balkyn is. She was eavesdropping, and she heard us talking about you."

I swallowed hard. "Has she told the king yet?"

She shook her head. "I don't know. But it's only a matter of time."

I pulled my knees up against my chest and wrapped my arms around them. "Dallas is on his way back here, but I don't know that I can get word to him before he leaves for Fifteen. In fact, I probably shouldn't. This is going to blow up, and I should keep him from the fire."

Eve's face crumpled. "I'm so sorry, Gwyn. I'd no idea Her Majesty was so curious about me."

"It's not your fault. You couldn't have guessed that she'd do something like that, and here you were, trying to help me. I hope you aren't in any trouble."

"I suppose we're all in a bit of trouble," Eve said. "But as I'm immortal and you're not, I'm more worried about you."

Hysterical laughter bubbled up from inside me. "As I suppose you should be." I willed the giggles to subside, but I had to wait them out. While I tried to calm myself, something Austin had said came back to me: *Enemies at every turn.* He'd been right. I loved Dallas, but our love was a minefield. Every step had the potential for catastrophe.

And here we were, about to blow sky-high.

I had to deal with this. I had to protect Dallas—from Balkyn, from his parents' wrath, from the lies we'd all told, from *me*.

"Thank you for letting me know." I smiled at Eve, trying to coax the guilty look from her face. "And when you next speak with Her Majesty, please tell her it was all my idea, everything to do with Balkyn. I don't want you, or the prince, for that matter, getting into trouble for trying to help my family."

Eve shook her head vehemently, her curls bouncing. "You aren't allowed to dismiss me, Gwyn. I'm not leaving you alone to deal with this."

I took a deep breath. "If you want to help me, leave me alone for now. I've got to think this through. I don't want to do anything before the prince is safely away from the palace again. I cannot put him at risk. Do you understand?"

"Yes. I'll keep a low profile while I wait to hear from you. But you should know the castle has eyes. Don't try to pull some trick, at least not without me. You won't get far enough to make it worth your while." She left without another word.

This was bloody it. My lies had caught up to me. It was time to face the music, or the vampires, as it were.

I had to let Dallas know that, no matter what, I'd had his best interests at heart. I could face anything as long as he knew I'd gone down fighting to protect him. That was the truth; that was *my* truth. I'd been the one to put him in harm's way. I'd be the one to save him from the wrath of the king.

I had to get the words down quickly, and get them right. I quickly got out a pen and paper. After pacing, lost in my thoughts for a few minutes, I knew what I had to say.

Dear Dallas,
I am so sorry, but I've just heard that news of who Balkyn really is has reached your parents. I can't even begin to apologize for all the trouble that I've dragged you into. And here we are, at the end of the competition. There couldn't be a worse time for this to come out.
And yet, it has.
I can't stop thinking that it's fate at work, tearing us apart. The

stars do not favor us, Dallas. Everything pushes against us, and has from the start.

And yet, I love you. I love you more than life itself.

It's that love which gives me the strength to do what's right. It's that love that teaches me to be selfless, even as it breaks my heart. I am no good for you. I would pretend to hate you, but you know me too well.

So I am asking you, if you love me, to let me go. Choose someone who can support your goals and dreams. Choose someone your family approves of. I cannot stand by and watch my feelings for you turn all your hopes for the settlements to dust. I cannot watch my love for you ruin your relationship with your father. I'm sorry for the trouble I've caused. And no words can express how sorry I am to lose you. But I know love because of you, and for that, I can never be sorry.

Who ever said doing the right thing would be easy?

I'll do what I can to spare you. You will forever have my heart.

Sincerely,

Your Gwyneth

I folded the letter and put it inside an envelope. I addressed it to the prince and left it on the nightstand.

And then I went to the window and waited.

CHAPTER 18
NOTHING LASTS FOREVER

THE WAITING TOOK SEVERAL HOURS. MY MAIDS CAME and went, fussing over me, bringing me tea and chicken soup, taking my temperature. I pretended to fall asleep so they'd leave me alone, even as I wanted to cling to them, to beg them to tell me everything was going to be all right.

Of course, I knew better than to ask. It wasn't ever going to be all right again.

I left the window open so I could hear what I could not see: Dallas's motorcade returning. I held my breath, wondering if the queen had already informed the king of my transgression. I worried that she and the king would corner Dallas with accusations and that he'd storm up here and try to rescue me. I worried, but I half wanted him to. I waited to hear the heavy fall of his boots in the hall outside my door.

But he never came.

Finally, in the early afternoon, I heard the cars leaving

again. I wondered what Blake and Dallas would talk about on their drive to Settlement 15—if she'd tell him I was sick or if she'd tell him the truth. Perhaps they wouldn't speak of me at all. Maybe they'd simply have a great time together, laughing and gossiping about Austin behind his back.

My heart careened in my chest, veering between hope for Dallas and pity for myself. But I'd made my bed, and it was time to lie in it.

I dressed in a plain black frock, pulling my hair into a lackluster bun. My plan was simple. First, check on my brother and see if he was still alive. I didn't know what, if anything, I could do for him. But I would try to protect him as best I could. Second, I'd go to the king and queen and tell them the truth. They already knew it, but they should hear it from me. I would fall on my sword, so to speak, and beg them to forgive Dallas and spare my brother. I wouldn't ask that much for myself. I wasn't naive enough to hope for salvation, given the circumstances.

I expected them to either march me down to the dungeons to share a cell with Balkyn or send me home immediately. Or worse. I knew the slim chance of them ever accepting me as their daughter-in-law was gone for good. A fresh round of tears threatened, but I forced myself to stop before I started. I'd let myself believe it was possible for Dallas and me to be together. My love for him had blinded me to the truth. But now everything I'd done was coming back to me—lying about my brother, the fact that I'd helped Benjamin Vale escape and then he'd killed those guards...

I saw little use in weeping over the inevitable. What was it Tariq had said? *We'll all be punished for our wrongs in the end, my dear.* That wanker had been right, for once.

I straightened my dress and took a deep breath. And then, with no idea if I'd ever return, I left the safety of my room.

❦

I'D ALMOST MADE IT DOWN THE HALL TO THE DUNGEON stairwell when a figure stepped out of the shadows. "Gwyneth?"

As he was tall and strapping, my heart caught in my throat. "Y-yes?" But Austin stepped into the light, and my heart sank. "Hello, Your Highness."

He frowned. "Where on earth do you think you're going?"

"Please keep your voice down." I looked around, relieved no guards were in sight. "I'm running an...errand."

Austin's eyebrow shot up a fraction. "An errand to the dungeons?"

I shrugged. "It's nothing interesting."

He leaned forward. "I think you'll need some backup on your 'errand.' I'll come with you. Dallas just bloody made me promise him again that I'd protect you."

"You saw him?"

"Yes. He was in and out of here. The production crew

said he didn't have time to see you, and he was in an uproar."

"But he left? With Blake?"

"Yes." Austin didn't look too happy about it.

"Okay." I exhaled. "Good."

"What's so good about it?"

"It means that he's where he's supposed to be. Now, if you'll excuse me, I have somewhere to be as well."

He stepped in front of me, blocking my path. "Not so fast. What's down there?" He jerked his thumb in the direction of the stairs.

I sighed. I didn't want to involve Austin, but as everyone else knew the truth, what more damage could I do? "My brother. He's your prisoner."

"Bloody hell, Gwyneth!"

"I've got to go see him. He's been down there for a while. Apparently, your mother just found out that he's my brother."

Austin raked a hand over his head. "This is genius, Gwyn. Just when I thought things couldn't get any worse for you."

Marching footsteps suddenly headed our way. They sounded as though they were coming from down the hall, near the grand foyer.

Austin and I looked at each other for a beat. "Here we go, getting worse again. C'mon. No one else needs to stumble across you and your errands today." We ran into the stairwell and hid in the dark alcove at the top of the landing. Austin quietly crouched, his weapon at the ready.

"You don't need to fight," I whispered. "These are *your* guards, for goodness' sake."

"And it's *my* duty to protect you, or my brother will see me staked."

"Carry on, then." Nervous laughter threatened, so I clutched my stomach to keep the laughs in.

The footsteps got closer and, much to my dismay, turned in to the stairwell. "We can bring him out, Your Highness," one of the sentinels said.

"I'd like to witness every second of this debacle." The king's voice was laced with a dull fury. "Why did no one tell me about his relation to the girl?"

"Because we didn't know, sire."

"Someone bloody knew. And when I find out who— who it was that chose to pledge their loyalty to my son instead of me—I will make an example of their head. On a very pretty, very sharp spike for all to see."

The guards glanced at each other as they descended the stairs. "Yes, Your Majesty."

I wanted to run at them, but Austin held me back. He waited until they'd gone all the way downstairs before he spoke. "We've got to get you out of here."

"I'm not leaving my brother. I'm a lot of things, but a coward isn't one of them."

"The only thing you'll be is dead if you don't listen to me."

I shook him off. "I'm not leaving him."

Austin cursed under his breath. "You're a stubborn one, aren't you? That's all right. I've been dealing with stubborn people my whole life." He put his ridiculously solid hands around me and started dragging me away.

"Let go of me!" I struggled, and he clamped his hand over my mouth. That didn't stop me from trying to yell, but it did muffle the effect.

Austin was as strong as an ox. He hauled me down the corridor easily, as if I weighed no more than a child's doll. But we met four more sentinels just as we made it to the grand foyer; they eyed us warily. "Your Highness." The shortest one bowed. "Thank you for finding this contestant. We've been looking for her."

"I found her first." Austin smiled at them easily. "I'll look after her."

The sentinel cleared his throat. "We're under strict instructions from the king to bring her to him directly."

"The king's busy at the moment. I just saw him." Austin moved to go around them.

The sentinels mirrored his movement, blocking his escape. "I'm sorry, Your Highness, but we've been ordered to take her into custody. You needn't trouble yourself."

Austin took a step back. His eyes glinted, and he looked a bit scary. "Oh, it's no trouble." The undertone in his voice was lethal.

At that moment, the queen floated down the stairs, her sky-blue silk dress billowing in waves around her. "Austin, my child, whatever are you doing?"

He nodded, keeping his hand firmly planted over my mouth. "Not too much, Mother. How're you?"

"I'm well. I've been doing a bit of snooping, actually.

I'm turning up all sorts of things lately. I see you've met Miss West."

"Yes, of course." He pulled me closer and clamped his hand down even more tightly over my mouth. "You're looking lovely, as usual. That color brings out your eyes." He grinned at her winningly. The baby of the family, Austin was obviously used to charming his mother into getting his way.

She put a hand over her heart at she reached the landing. "Oh, sweetheart, it's so nice to have you at the palace. I've missed you. You do always know how to light up my day."

"Years of practice, Mother." He smiled tightly. "I don't suppose you want to light up my day by calling off your dogs?"

Her sapphire-blue eyes sparkled at her son. "You think your father would be amenable to that?"

"Since when was he amenable to anything I did?"

"Darling, don't be like that..."

As they went back and forth, I noticed Eve sneaking down the hallway. She put a finger to her lips. She slid closer, eavesdropping on the conversation and inspecting the sentinels' aggressive postures. They were ready to pounce should Austin make the slightest move.

I will try to help you, she thought inside my head. I wished I could respond to her, to tell her to run away—it was too late for me. Boots marched down the hall from the direction of the dungeons, and I looked to Eve, my eyes pleading for her to run. With one last nod, she took off around the corner, toward the northern part of the castle.

The Black Guard marched into the grand foyer. Two guards in the middle held Balkyn up. He was so pale and wasted, he looked as though he could barely stand. His filthy white T-shirt and tan pants hung from his gaunt frame. He looked scarier than the vampires who surrounded him.

"Brother." It came out muffled, and Austin finally removed his hand from my face.

"Don't say too much," he whispered gently. He slowly released me as he eyed the guards. "And don't run away. There isn't much point."

I nodded, then reached toward my brother. "Balkyn."

His eyes could barely focus as he turned in my direction. "Is that a witch, or is it my sister?" He cackled as his gaze finally found me. "Or is it both?"

"We should get them to a private room before the cameras find us and hear all of this," Austin reminded his mother.

"Of course."

The king stepped out from behind his guard, looking from Balkyn to me in disgust. "I don't bloody care who hears it. Let them see how we deal with traitors."

The queen held out her hand for him. "Come, dear. We mustn't undo all the good work we've done over the past few months."

With a final, hateful look in my direction, the king took her hand. "To the throne room," he commanded.

Austin leaned toward me as we followed the king and

queen. "I won't leave you. I'll make them understand that this is all a mistake."

"It's not a mistake," I hissed. "That's my brother. He's a rebel. He hates vampires, to the point where he'd literally rather starve to death than eat your food. He's been here since the rebels captured me and almost killed Dallas. There's no way to 'spin' this. The only thing that's about to get spun are both my and my brother's heads, around the floor of the throne room after they're chopped off."

He gave me a quick look. "I'm not going to let that happen."

"You and what bloody army?"

He didn't say anything after that.

Balkyn was behind me, but he didn't say another word as we made our way to the throne room. I wondered what he was thinking or if he was so dehydrated that he was hallucinating. I swallowed hard as we reached the large room, golden thrones gleaming on a dais. The last time I'd been here, Dallas had been forced to kill Benjamin Vale because of my folly. Oh, how I wished my prince were here now! Even if it were only to say goodbye. I closed my eyes and pictured his handsome face, remembering what it felt like to sink my hands into his thick hair. Every moment we'd shared flashed before me.

By the time Austin deposited me in the middle of the room to be judged, I felt calmer. It was better that Dallas wasn't here. He wouldn't suffer by witnessing this. Still, I felt his presence. It was as though his love had marked me. He'd become a part of me that nothing—not time, not distance, not the fierce burning of his father's hate—could take away.

I'd had my happiness; whatever came next, I could face it. If Balkyn and I were punished now, we would go together forever into the hereafter. Perhaps with eternity on my side, I could convince my brother to forgive me.

And at least, if we were gone, Dallas would have no more trouble. He wouldn't have anything to hide, and he wouldn't have to lie for me anymore. He could marry one of the other girls, someone the king and queen approved of, and maybe he'd have a chance at happiness, real happiness.

I faced the king and queen, and I was ready. The king looked at me with hate in his eyes, and I understood him perfectly. I forgave him.

I held my head high, and I curtsied.

And then I waited for judgment.

CHAPTER 19
I'M STILL WAITING

"THEY'VE CALLED FOR THE COURT," AUSTIN WHISPERED to me. "It won't be long now."

Vampire lords and ladies filed into the room, taking seats along the wall, all the better to watch the spectacle. I'd seen most of them before, the first time I was here, on the night that Benjamin Vale was killed, and they'd also attended the royal gala. They must have all lived at the castle, but they stayed out of sight of the contestants during the day. They peered at my brother and me but said nothing, patiently waiting for the royals to proceed.

The king and queen spoke in low tones, periodically looking in our direction. I stole a glance at Balkyn, but his eyes were closed, his head lolled back. Two guards held him up—I couldn't tell if he was conscious.

"Balkyn." I kept my voice so low, only Austin and the nearby guards could hear us. *Balkyn.*

His eyes snapped open.

"Are you awake?"

He scoffed at me. "I am now."

His skin was a ghastly color, a sickly yellow, and his eyes still seemed to have trouble focusing. "Do you know where you are?"

"Yes, unfortunately." He blinked, looking around. "Where's your vampire? I don't see him with this lot. Has he abandoned you already?"

"He's none of your concern. I just want you to be ready. The king and queen have discovered you're my brother. They're about to—"

"They're about to put your heads on spikes." Austin grunted. "You'd best be quiet."

"I've nothing to say to her, anyway." Balkyn looked away in disgust.

"A real charmer, your brother," Austin whispered.

I groaned but immediately silenced myself as the king stood. He bowed to the court, then turned to face us.

"It has come to my attention that this prisoner—this *rebel prisoner*—is related to one of the Pageant's contestants." The lords and ladies gasped, whispering to each other and staring. "His sister is a girl who has come to live under our roof, eat our food, and spend time amongst us. Her brother is a rebel. Not only is he a rebel, he's also a leader of the rebel army, captured by my son and thrown into our dungeons, where he's been kept prisoner for weeks."

The audience whispered some more until the king cleared his throat and continued. "This fact has been kept from me by members of the Black Guard, our staff, and the Prince himself." King Black paced stiffly across the dais. "To say that I'm disappointed, as well as disgusted, is too mellow a description—"

The door to the throne room was thrust open, and Tariq burst in, his chest heaving. He was followed closely by Rose, Mira Kinney's harried assistant, as well as several network executives. "Your Highness. I've just had word about this terrible situation. I'm so sorry for the interruption, but we're still filming the final hours of the competition—"

"How *dare* you interrupt me!" the king roared. "I'm holding court. Not another word, Tariq."

"But Your Highness—"

"Seize him. Seize all of them." The king snapped his fingers, and several members of the Black Guard surrounded the humans at the door.

"There we go, Father. Don't be shy," Austin called cheerfully. "Let them see your true colors. The humans at home were starting to think you might actually be likable. You need to set them straight."

The queen gave her son a sharp look, which even I could tell meant *shut your mouth*. But Austin paid no attention. He gleefully eyed Tariq and the others. "Why don't we have a meal together, Father? I'm with you. Down with the humans, the human-lovers, and all the race traitors! Time to circle the wagon, I say. Let's show the settlers and the rebels what we're really capable of, once and for all. That will keep them in line better than placating them with a human princess, I'll bet."

The king frowned at his son. "I haven't missed you."

Austin's smile didn't falter. "That makes two of us, then."

"Enough. These two humans—the rebel and his traitor-sister—will be sentenced shortly. I will spare my older son this debacle, but I won't spare the settlements. It will be filmed for them to watch. They need to understand what happens to those who would betray us." He nodded toward Tariq. "The competition will go on as planned, as you wish. But there will be one less contestant. You will bring a crew here to film their sentencing and judgment. Let the citizens see what befalls traitors to the throne."

The king motioned to the guards surrounding Balkyn and me. "Take them to a holding cell so that we may prepare."

Austin squeezed my shoulder before they dragged me off. "Don't worry, my lady. It's not over yet."

"It's seems a bit dire, though." Again, nervous laughter bubbled inside me.

"Just a bit." Austin grinned. "And so you know, I didn't mean what I said. About dining on the humans. Maybe just Tariq, though he's a bit perfumey for my taste."

"Mine, too." I giggled. I could feel the hysterics threatening.

He released me. "Off you go, then. I'll be waiting for you. A promise is a promise, after all."

I nodded, my heart pounding, as the guards dragged me away.

CHAPTER 20
INJURED IN DOUBT

THE DUNGEONS SEEMED DIFFERENT WHEN I WAS actually inside a cell. "This isn't as bad as I imagined," I called to my brother. "It's quite cozy." I picked at my thin blanket.

"I'm really not quite sure why you're still *chatting* at me." I couldn't see his face, but I knew Balkyn was sporting a sour frown. "It's a bit desperate of you."

"I suppose it is, but that's understandable, under the circumstances. Don't you think?"

Balkyn snorted. "I think you should've listened to me before. Nothing good can come from mixing with them. Look at where you landed, Miss High-and-Mighty."

"I'm next to my brother, who I thought I'd lost years ago," I mused. "I don't see this as a terrible predicament. I see it as a blessing."

"We're about to be publicly beheaded by the vampire king. Do you really feel blessed?"

I sighed. "That's not what I'm talking about, and you

know it. Can't you speak to me as you used to? As your sister, your family?"

"I told you." Balkyn's voice was strangled. "You're no longer my sister."

"And yet here we are, together at the very end." No matter what he said, his presence still comforted me. "You cannot accept that fate has given us a second chance?"

"I don't know that fate has given me anything other than a headache these last five years." Balkyn's laugh sounded hollow.

"I saw Mother, Winnie, and Remy recently. They're doing well. Winnie and Remy are growing up, Balkyn. There's so smart and curious. They're so, so good."

He cleared his throat. "I'm glad for it."

"What about Father? What does fate have in store for him?" I laced my hands together, praying that he would tell me something—anything.

"He's sick, Gwyn, like I've told you. The last I saw him, his fever had been burning him up for weeks. There was nothing we could do."

"I wish... I wish he were here." Tears sprang to my eyes, and I willed them away. I wouldn't spend the precious time I had left blubbering. "There's plenty of medicine here, and doctors. We could get him help. He could be comfortable."

"You know Father. He's tough. If he's still alive, you can bet he's doing just fine. And if he didn't make it..."

"Then we'll see him again soon." I put my palm flat upon the wall, as if I could touch my brother through it.

"Yes," Balkyn said softly. "Yes, we will."

Footsteps echoed down the hall. "You two—on your feet." A gruff-looking sentinel unlocked our doors. "They're waiting for you."

Heart in my throat, I climbed from my cot. *It's almost time.* Two additional guards went in to help my brother. They practically carried him up the stairs. My heart thudded as we climbed out of the dungeons. Each step I took, I wondered—how many many minutes of my life remained? I panicked, because I didn't want to waste a second. *Dallas.* I needed to feel him with me now, to give me strength.

We made it up the stairs and into the hall. I followed the sentinels, concentrating—not on my surroundings—but remembering Dallas's touch as he brushed the hair from my face. How he'd held me during the one precious night we'd spent together. How much I loved the way he smelled, the feel of my face pressed against his chest. I remembered, and I tried to be brave as we were marched back to the throne room.

The king and queen waited, as did Austin and the vampire court. Tariq and a film crew stood ready in the wings, their cameras already set up and rolling. The royal emissary was pale except for two hectic spots of color in his cheeks. His eyes darted around my brother and me, as if he still couldn't quite believe what he was seeing.

The room had been slightly rearranged. Various tall ceremonial weapons were lined up, on gleaming display near the thrones. A large, blood-red Oriental rug had been placed in the center of the room. Balkyn and I were led onto the rug, squarely in front of the king and queen.

A sentinel stepped forward as trumpets sounded. "Introducing His Royal Majesty, King Reginald Black, Crown King of the United Royal Settlements. Introducing Her Royal Majesty, Queen Serena Black, Crown Queen of the United Royal Settlements."

The king and queen each bowed slightly, then the king stepped forward. "We are here to sentence these two humans for treason. The prisoner is a rebel. Do you admit to your crimes, rebel?"

Balkyn lifted his chin. "I admit to no crimes. But I'll die a rebel and with no regrets."

The king's eyes flicked over him with distaste. He turned to me, and the distaste turned to clear disgust. "And what say you, Miss West? Do you admit that while you were a guest in our home, you knew that your brother was both a rebel—a sworn enemy of the royal family—as well as a prisoner here?"

I lifted my chin. "Yes, Your Highness. Balkyn West is a rebel and a prisoner. And he is my brother, until my last breath."

"Do you admit to *lying* to your hosts, the royal family, about this? Do you admit to hiding the truth?"

"Yes, Your Highness, I did lie. I lied to protect not only my brother but also myself. It was a coward's choice. I accept my punishment fully."

The queen stepped forward and cleared her throat. "Did you also lie to protect someone else, child?"

"Well—well, yes, Your Majesty." I didn't dare speak

his name, lest his father's fury become focused on him. "But the point is, it was my idea to lie. I didn't want anyone in the palace to know the rebel prisoner was my brother. I didn't want to hurt my chances in the competition."

The queen turned to her husband as if to say something, but the king ignored her. He stepped past her to the front of the dais. "Enough of your excuses," he said. "It was a selfish choice, Miss West. Worse than that, a traitorous one." He stared around the room, taking everyone's measure. "I've heard everything necessary. It's time for their judgments."

I glanced at Balkyn, who stared straight ahead.

"Husband, wait—" the queen said.

But the king would not wait. "I sentence both of these humans to death."

I sucked in a deep breath. Balkyn reached for me and took my hand in his. Shocked, I looked his way again. This time, his gaze met mine, the ghost of a smile on his lips.

"Guards, prepare them." A sentinel put his hands on my shoulders as the king reached for a large axe, etched in gold. Although my brother's hand around mine warmed my heart, a wave of dread crashed through me as the blade of the axe glinted in the afternoon light.

The king descended the steps and stopped before us. "Kneel."

Time stopped for a moment. My heart thundered. This was all happening so fast...how could I prepare for my life to end?

How could I say goodbye?

But there was no time. Hand in hand, Balkyn and I dropped to our knees. Balkyn bowed his head, waiting. I did the same. I didn't want to spend my last moments looking at that axe.

"You're no coward, sister," Balkyn said quietly. "The last words I speak on this earth should be the truth."

I squeezed his hand. "I love you, brother. I'll see you on the other side."

The room grew silent as death. I held my breath, waiting for the blade. But then heavy footsteps thundered across the stone floor. "Not so fast! A word, Father," a familiar, beloved voice said.

I tentatively peered up, wondering if I was already dead and heaven was real, after all.

Dallas swept into the throne room, his cape flying behind him. Despite all my proclamations about being ready to say goodbye and carrying him in my heart, I almost fainted in relief at the sight of him. "I've just come from my trip to Settlement Fifteen, which I cut short when I heard news of what's happened here. You can't do this—you can't sentence Miss West and her brother to death. And you certainly can't televise it." He snapped his fingers at Tariq, who in turn motioned for the cameras to stop filming.

"Don't you dare turn those cameras off!" The king raised himself to his considerable height.

"Trust me, Father, you don't want word of this getting out. There'll be a massive revolt. I've seen it for myself."

The queen quickly descended the steps, coming next to her husband. "Listen to him. He has news."

"He's trying to protect the girl, which is what brought all the trouble in the first place."

She narrowed her eyes at the king. "Let him speak. You cut me off earlier. It might be in your best interests to hear out at least *one* of your family members. We might have something important to tell you, darling."

The king looked a bit cowed. "Fine. Tariq, leave us."

Tariq and the cameras were gone in an instant, without a peep of argument.

The king turned to Dallas. "You have one minute. Speak."

The muscle in Dallas's jaw jumped. "First, I'd like to get Miss West off the floor." He practically shoved the guard behind me out of the way and reached for my hands. He gently pulled me to my feet. Emotions swirled in his eyes—regret, relief, anger, sadness. "Miss West. My apologies for my father's behavior." He briefly took me in his arms and kissed the top of my head.

When I looked up, the king had turned red. He still gripped the axe tightly. "There's no need to apologize to *her*. She's a rebel-lover, son. A traitor."

"Just because her brother's a rebel—and her father, I might mention—it doesn't make her a traitor. Whether or not she loves them is none of your bloody business." Dallas held out a hand to Balkyn. My brother looked up at him, a mixture of surprise and regret playing out on his face.

He accepted the prince's hand and shakily rose to his feet.

I supported Balkyn against me as the prince turned to once more face the king. "Put the axe away, Father. There will be no executions today."

The king visibly stiffened, still clutching the weapon. "You haven't said one thing to change my mind, son."

Dallas sighed. "Then let me speak. But put that axe away first. You've scared the woman I love enough for one lifetime. I won't tolerate it another moment."

CHAPTER 21
I WAS LOST...

IT TOOK EVERY OUNCE OF SELF-CONTROL THE KING possessed to civilly return the axe to its display case. He stiffly sat on his throne, waiting for his older son to explain himself.

The queen patted his hand, as if she were proud of his restraint, but the king refused to acknowledge her touch. He looked longingly at the axe.

"As you know, I was headed to Settlement Fifteen with Miss Kensington this afternoon," Dallas said. "I was astonished by what I saw as we traveled through the settlements. The citizens were out by the thousands. Many of them had signs. *All* of them were cheering. And they were cheering for Miss West."

My jaw dropped. "For me?"

"Yes, for you." Dallas motioned for a guard to bring a chair, and he gently helped Balkyn into it. Then he took my hand, lacing his fingers through mine. "The network didn't want us to tell the finalists, but the nation is united. You're the people's choice. They want you as their princess, Gwyneth. The polls are showing almost unanimous approval for you, outside of the other girls' home settlements. There's been rallies all week, candle-light vigils... It's quite impressive." He smiled, and it was like the sun coming out after a long, cold winter. "After your episode aired, when the people saw you at the clinic, and they saw *us* together, they knew. It was obvious to everyone that I'd made my choice. Mira didn't want the other girls to know. She didn't want them to get dispir-ited, and she also wanted to make the final days of the contest dramatic. She wants the ratings to be sky-high, of course."

"You might've mentioned that before." Austin grimaced, his gaze veering between his father and his brother. "Things were about to get a bit...close." He eyed the sharp edge of the axe.

Dallas's face turned stormy. "Do not speak to me. You've failed me for the last time, brother."

Austin rolled his eyes. "You are getting a bit dramatic in your old age. Her neck's still intact."

"Barely." Dallas's voice was ice.

"Don't be so harsh," I whispered. "He did try to save me."

"He did a very bad job, so far as I can tell."

"I'm losing patience." The king struggled to sit still in his seat. "Despite what you've said, I see no reason to spare these two. In fact, her popularity will bring more attention to the topic. Treason won't be tolerated, not by anyone."

"Beheading the settlement's choice won't be tolerated either, Father. Not by the citizens and not by me." His gaze raked over the king. "Remember why you agreed to this contest in the first place. You did it to bring excitement and unity to the settlements. You've succeeded. If we stop now—if we make an example of her in such a brutal way—there's no turning back from an uprising. We can't betray the settlements like that and expect them to take it."

The king shot to his feet. "But we're the ones who've been betrayed. She's a rebel sympathizer, living in our home. Son, your feelings have blinded you. This girl has deceived you."

"I knew about her brother all along. I'm the one who put him in the dungeons."

"That doesn't matter." The king hesitated. "What I mean is, she's deceived you into wanting to protect her. She's using you, son."

Dallas pulled me protectively against him. "That's not true. Gwyneth and I are in love."

Austin stepped forward. "She does love him, Father. The loon admitted as much to me."

The king pointed at his sons. "You're both young and naive. Egotistical, too. You're also wealthy, powerful, and good looking. Of course you think she loves you. You don't understand that a person can have no feelings for you and act as if they do. People in power are used all the time. This girl's no different. She wanted to protect her brother. When it comes down to it, that's where her loyalty lies."

The queen cleared her throat. "I have something to say." She smiled at Dallas, then frowned at her husband. "You're wrong, dear. And I have proof."

"I'm not really sure how you *prove* such a thing, but—"

"I have a letter she wrote to our son." From the depths of her skirts, she pulled out the envelope I'd addressed to Dallas. Her sapphire gaze found mine. "Forgive me for going through your things, child. But when I discovered that your brother had been down in the dungeons for some time, it made me question what I'd seen growing between you and my son. I doubted you."

Unable to speak, I nodded.

"But I no longer doubt Miss West." She held up the letter. "She tells our son in this note that she does, in fact, love our son—more than life itself. She also says that she would have him choose someone else, someone we would approve of, Reginald. She said that she didn't want her love to destroy Dallas's relationship with you, as she feared the news about her brother might. She vowed to *protect* him. That is love. It is not your son's ego. There's no guile to it." She handed the letter to Dallas. "I believe this is yours."

"Thank you, Mother." He tucked it away. "So, Father, what say you?"

The king's gaze traveled over my brother, then to me, my hand entwined with his son's. "I would not choose this for you."

Dallas straightened his spine. "But will you support my choice?"

Everyone stared at the king. The queen's eyes shone brightly as we waited.

The king nodded stiffly. "Your bride is your choice. If she loves you and does not deceive you, I will support you, son."

Dallas hugged me as Austin clapped. The queen beamed at her husband, then at us.

"But there's still a problem." The king made sure our humble celebration didn't last long. "Her brother. No rebel who attacks my family shall be allowed to live. I'm afraid I can't spare him."

"Your Highness, *please*." I fell to my knees, begging. "He fought you before he knew you, to protect our land and our family from invaders."

"He said he will die a rebel, with no regrets." Did I imagine it, or did the king's eyes twinkle? He seemed pleased to have me on my knees, near tears again. "And so he shall."

"Father, no. No matter his transgressions, he's Gwyneth's flesh and blood. He will remain our prisoner if he must."

"He will do no such thing. He's a liability, Dallas. He knows too much about us, and his sister makes us weak. He must die. If you cannot accept that, I have only one other offer."

Dallas's face darkened. "What." He didn't bother to make it sound like a question.

"We must turn him."

Balkyn's face crumpled with fury, and I gripped his hand. He was too weak to fight or even to pretend to make a run for it, and his feelings were plain on his face. He knew he couldn't outrun being turned into a vampire, which he considered a fate worse than death.

His tortured gaze locked with mine. "Please. No," he whispered.

"I agree, Father." Dallas bowed his head before the king.

I looked at him, aghast. "Dallas, no!"

"He's a threat to us, Gwyneth. A threat to you. As a vampire, his rebel ties will be severed forever. It's the only way." He nodded at his father. "And I'll go one step further—I'll turn him myself."

The king's face relaxed into a smile. He looked as though he'd won something.

"I'll have the prisoner cleaned up. We can do it tonight. It's best to have him taken care of before there's any chance of the outside world finding out about him."

"Why don't we take care of it now?" the king asked.

"I'd prefer to change him outside, in the garden, at twilight. We'll make a ceremony out of it. Like the good old days, to mark the birth of a new member of the vampire family. Guards, take him. Make sure he's bathed. He smells of filth and rot at the moment."

The guards dragged my brother away, his head hanging in despair. I knew what he was thinking: the axe was a better fate.

Dallas held out his hand for me. But even under the king's watchful eye, I ignored the offer. I climbed to my feet, lifting my chin high. "I'd like to be at the ceremony, Your Highness."

"Of course. I would expect nothing less." Dallas nodded. "You should return to your chambers, Gwyneth, and have a bath. You've had a rough afternoon. Guards, take her."

Dumbstruck, I had no response. The prince bowed to me one last time. The sentinels marched me off, my heart racing, thoughts spinning, and heart breaking yet again.

CHAPTER 22
...I AM FOUND

I KEPT MY HEAD DOWN ON THE WAY TO MY ROOM. Shaye was back, and so was Blake—because her trip had been cut short. I prayed I wouldn't bump into any of the other girls, or worse yet, Tariq. He'd witnessed my lowest hour, and now he knew my secret.

I made it inside my chambers without detection. I bathed, washing my hair repeatedly, as if I could wash the horror of what had happened—and what would happen —away, and rinse it down the drain. If only.

The sun crossed the sky, heading further west fast, too fast. It would be evening soon. My heart, worn out, skittered in my chest. Why had Dallas agreed to change Balkyn? Was he doing it for the reason his father wanted —as a punishment? Or did he think it less cruel to let Balkyn live as a vampire, as opposed to a lifelong prisoner?

I didn't know. All I knew was that my brother was broken by the sentence. Even though he'd seemed to forgive me and had certainly been grateful when Dallas first appeared in the throne room, Balkyn did not want to become a vampire. His closely held beliefs would never allow him to see the change as anything but a curse. This was worse than a death sentence for him.

And the trouble was, Dallas knew that. He *had* to.

Why had he volunteered to turn my brother into a vampire?

I wanted to go to Dallas, to find out what was going on inside his head. But I didn't dare leave my room. I'd barely escaped the king's large, shiny axe blade. I had no intention of risking getting near it again.

Still, my heart raced and my thoughts swirled as I dried my hair. My brother, I had to save my brother...

A knock on the door jarred me from my thoughts. "Miss? It's me. I've just come with your tea." Evangeline bustled into the room, setting up the tea service. "We've had word that you're to attend a private ceremony tonight with the royal family. Are you feeling better?"

"Yes," I lied, my voice hoarse. "Much."

She peered at me, her pretty face puckered in worry. "I don't mean to pry, but is everything quite all right? All the staff is in an uproar. No one knows why the prince cut his visit to Fifteen so short. He never even made it there. And now, this ceremony..."

I sighed, gratefully accepting the tea she offered. "I don't know what to tell you, Evangeline. The prince came back because he had urgent family business to attend to. I don't know what the ceremony tonight's all about." I hated lying, but I wanted to shield her from the truth.

She nodded. "I'll bring you some food, then. You won't have time to dine with the other ladies. And I'll send Bria and Bettina along to do your hair and makeup."

"O-okay. Thank you."

She curtsied and left. Realizing my hand was shaking, I hastily put the tea cup down. And then I went to the window, watching the sun as it set much too fast.

❧

BRIA HAD JUST PUT THE FINISHING TOUCHES ON MY hair and Bettina had just packed away the makeup crate when another knock sounded.

A sentinel waited. "I'm here for Miss West. It's time for the ceremony."

"Yes, of course. She'll just be a moment." Evangeline closed the door and came closer. "Are you ready?"

I nodded, trying to quell the tremors shooting through me. "Of course." I peered at the three of them. They all looked worried, their faces pinched in concern. "What's the matter?"

Bettina patted my hand. "It's just that you're deathly pale underneath your makeup."

"And trembling," Bria added.

"And you seem distracted." Evangeline bit her lip. "Everything's going to be okay, miss. Even if it's not okay."

"T-thank you." Even my voice was shaking. I'd best keep my mouth shut.

"I wish you'd tell us what was going on." Bria frowned at me.

"But she cannot, and we mustn't add to her trouble," Evangeline scolded. She squeezed my shoulder. "We'll be back tonight for your turn-down service. We'll see you soon."

I nodded, unable to say what I was thinking: *I'm afraid for my brother. Don't leave me. Help me stop time.* Instead, I smiled at them and rose unsteadily to my feet. "Thank you. For everything." Without another word, I went to meet the sentinel.

He was silent as he led me down the back stairs to the western lawn. It was almost twilight, the sun sinking below the horizon. We navigated a path lit by elegant lanterns to a stone courtyard surrounded by high hedges. In the center, a fire roared in the fire pit. A platform stood at the far end of the garden. I swallowed hard as I saw the king and queen seated on it, gracing their thrones. The vampire lords and ladies milled about, dressed in their finery, chatting amongst themselves. They made the gathering look like a cocktail party, not what it really was: a celebration to mark the end of my brother's life.

Shaking, I stepped toward the king and queen. I curtsied. They nodded in return. The king's face was relaxed and open—he was enjoying this. The queen watched me with her sapphire-blue eyes, the expression on her face unreadable. I quickly moved to the side of the courtyard, wishing the large hedges could swallow me whole.

A small band began to play as smoke from the fire

rose into the air. One of the vampire ladies laughed, a shrill sound that made my skin crawl. *They're having fun.* A sense of anticipation filled the air. Waiters in tuxedos served the crowd silver goblets. One of the vampire lords strode toward the king and queen, holding out his chalice in a toast. "To the Royal Family, and the creation of a new family member. May you continue to rule the settlements in peace and prosperity. Long live the king!"

"Long live the king!" the crowd chanted. They all drank as the king stood and took a bow.

Moments later, Austin strode into the courtyard. He wore a ceremonial uniform, cape flying out behind him. He bowed to his parents. "The prince is on his way, along with the prisoner. It won't be long now." He accepted a goblet from a passing waiter and held it forth. "To tonight's ceremony, and to the settlements! To peace and prosperity for centuries to come! I'll drink to that!" He grinned as the crowd cheered, then took a large swallow from his drink.

Austin's gaze flicked to me as I tried to hide on the outskirts. He winked. Then he sauntered off, talking to the lords and ladies, regaling them with stories of the North as the music continued to merrily play. If only I could feel festive. Instead, dread filled me as I watched the revelers. When would Balkyn arrive? What was my brother thinking right now? And what about Dallas?

I sank back against the hedges, willing myself to calm down. But something ice cold—someone—grabbed my wrist. *Don't say a word.* As it was spoken inside my head, I knew it could only be one person.

Eve dragged me back through the bush. Its springy leaves scratched my face as its branches scraped me, nearly tearing my dress. "What the bloody hell are you doing?" I whispered as she finally got me out the other side. I picked the leaves and twigs from my hair.

She nodded at me, curls springing. "That's a lovely way to thank me."

"Thank you for *what*—for getting me beheaded? The king'll happily get out his axe again, once he realizes I've skipped out of the ceremony!"

"You can thank me for getting Dallas back to the castle, for one thing." She tugged on my wrist, marching me away from the gathering and out into the grounds.

I dug my heels in, too afraid to flee from the ceremony. "Dallas is about to turn my brother. I'm not feeling very grateful, I'm afraid."

"Well come on, then. Don't fight me." Eve snorted as she pulled on me, urging me forward. "We've got to hurry. There isn't much time."

"Time for *what?*" I cried, but she didn't say another word as she hustled me away. The music and the smell of smoke from the fire faded away into the background.

I was quite out of breath as we crested a small hill, but she kept dragging me toward the tree line. "Eve, what the bloody hell—" But hooves thundered nearby, cutting off my question. Before I could argue further, Dallas shot out of the forest on Maeve, the beautiful white mare. He held the reins to another white horse who galloped slightly behind. I gasped as they drew closer—Balkyn was with him. He held onto Dallas for dear life as they headed for us at a breakneck speed.

I clapped my hand over my heart. "Dallas! Balkyn!"

Maeve whinnied as the prince tugged her reigns and brought her to a stop. The other horse pulled up behind them. "Eve. Take Balkyn and follow us closely. I don't know how long my brother can hold off the court with his stories. We have to hurry."

Eve quickly helped Balkyn down from the horse. I ran to him. My brother pulled me in for a hug, his arms stronger than I would've expected from his frail appearance. "Thank you for this." He released me and hurried with Eve, climbing up behind her into the saddle.

Eve winked at me as she adjusted the reins. "Want to thank me now?"

I nodded. "Y-yes."

Dallas looked down at me, his eyes stormy. "I'm sorry for the secrecy, but I didn't want to put you at any more risk. This is our one chance to get him out of here alive."

I choked back a sob. "You don't have to apologize to me. Not ever."

He held out his hand for me as Maeve whinnied again. "Shall we?"

There was only one answer. I reached for his hand. "Yes."

"WHERE ARE WE TAKING HIM?" I HAD TO SHOUT OVER the wind and Maeve's pounding hooves.

Dallas urged the mare on faster, darting in and out of the trees. "He told me where I could find his men."

"But Dallas." I clutched him even tighter. "Is that safe? I trust my brother, but the other rebels... They won't want to let you go."

"I have Balkyn's word they will, and that is good enough for me. "

I had a thousand objections, but the wind and my better judgment kept me quiet. He would save my brother, no matter the cost. Even as fear for Dallas's safety bubbled inside me, I pressed my face against his back, hugging him, loving him with every cell of my body. He was the bravest person I'd ever known.

I held him tighter. I wouldn't waste another moment.

We rode further into the woods, the darkness gathering. Eve and Dallas slowed the horses to a walk.

"It's about a mile from here," Balkyn said. "We should stop. I can make it on foot. You do not need to take me."

Eve shook her head. "He's too weak. I will deliver him, Your Highness. You and Gwyneth should wait here —you mustn't risk it."

Dallas stopped Maeve and climbed off. "I'll bring him from here. Eve, take my horse. Keep Gwyneth safe—go to the meeting place. I'll be there shortly."

I scrambled down after him. "Dallas, no!"

He turned on his heel, cape flying, and clasped my hands. "I will be fine. Your family is my family, now. We look after each other."

My eyes filled with tears. "Let *me* take him. They won't hurt a human. You, on the other hand—you're the prize they're after."

"They won't be getting their prize today. Go with Eve. That's an order." He leaned closer, eyes fiery. "I will come back to you."

"How do you know?" I asked hoarsely.

"Because I will always come back to you."

I threw myself at him, wrapping my arms around his neck and pulling him in for a deep, passionate kiss. Electricity coursed through me as he sank his hands into my hair and pulled me closer, our bodies molding together.

"Blimey," I heard Eve say, "are they breathing through their noses? That's quite a trick!"

Dallas and I broke apart, chests heaving. He grinned, tapping me on the chin, bringing my gaze even with his. "I'll see you soon."

I opened my mouth, but before I could even speak, he winked at me. "I love you, too."

"Sister." Balkyn climbed down from the horse and hugged me again, more gently this time. "I'm so sorry for—"

"No." I shook my head vehemently. "No apologies. I thank the gods we got to see each other again. I love you, Balkyn."

His eyes shone with tears as he released me and stepped back. "And I love you, sister. Always have, always will. We'll see each other again, someday. Even if it's in the next life."

"Yes."

I couldn't say anything else. I could only watch as he climbed behind Dallas and they rode away, deeper into the dark forest.

※

EVE GUIDED MAEVE OUT OF THE TREES AND TOWARD A small hill. We could see the palace, lights winking in the distance.

I tried not to think about the rebels, and whether they would let Dallas go. I would end up a blubbering mess, which would solve nothing.

"What will the king do?" I asked Eve, in an attempt to distract myself from the minutes ticking past.

"Well, I suppose he'll throw a bit of a fit." Eve frowned as she looked at the castle. "But in the end, what *can* he do? Dallas is his son. He loves him. He'll have to accept that they don't see eye to eye on certain things, is all."

I winced. "Helping a rebel prisoner escape and lying to his father about it—in front of an audience—is a bit worse than not seeing eye to eye, I think."

Eve shrugged. "Vampires live a long life. Things that seem catastrophic to humans might be more of a blip to our kind."

"I hope this is only a 'blip,' but I'm a bit skeptical, I'm afraid. My head was almost on a spike earlier today, so everything *does* seem a bit catastrophic." I rubbed my neck.

"Yeah, that'll do it." My friend grinned at me.

I reached for her hand and squeezed it. "I can't believe you got Dallas back to the castle in time, and did all this to save my brother. Thank you for everything. You're so brave, Eve."

"Brave or stupid—we'll see what His Majesty has in store for *me*."

Maeve suddenly whinnied. I stroked her mane. "What is it, girl?"

Hooves pounded nearby and Dallas rounded the corner, his horse a flash of white against the darkening sky. I put a hand over my heart. *He's safe.* "Dallas!"

He slowed the mare. "Your brother's safe, Gwyneth. The men who took him said they have medical supplies and food. They're bringing him back to a secure camp. He's going to be okay."

"They let you go?"

"Your brother vouched for me, and said that he

wouldn't return to the army unless they gave their word to allow me safe passage. They didn't hesitate."

"Thank God." He got close enough so I could make out his handsome face in the fading light. "Thank you. Of course, I can never thank you enough."

He grinned, then held out a hand for me. "I expect we'll have some time to test that theory. At least, I hope we do."

I climbed up behind him, wrapping my arms around his strong body. "I'm not sure what your family will have to say about...us, not after everything that's happened. And we have to make sure your father doesn't take his wrath out on Eve. She's saved the day, again."

"We don't need to worry about my father—not for Eve, not for us." He turned to Eve. "If I haven't said it lately, thank you. This would have been impossible without you."

She shrugged, but I could tell she was pleased. "It's nothing."

"I'm sorry, but I don't understand. Why don't we need to worry about your father? He was waiting for you to turn Balkyn, and he was excited about it. I could tell. So not only did you let my brother go, you made your father—the king—look a fool. I think we should all be at least a bit worried." I instinctively rubbed my throat again. "Maybe more than a bit."

"He can't harm me, or go against my wishes. Not anymore."

Eve and I waited for him to go on. "How's that?" she asked, as she readied Maeve.

Dallas sighed. "Remember I told you, Gwyneth, that the people in the settlements were rooting for you?"

"Yes."

"It's not just you they're excited about. Mira Kinney told me my approval ratings are one-hundred percent. The settlers are united behind *us*, Gwyneth. They're calling for me to rule. If my father makes a move against me, I could start a revolution. His empire's too precious to him—he won't risk it."

Eve climbed into her saddle and we set off toward the palace. "Is he aware of all this?"

"Not yet." Dallas lifted his chin. "But he will be. And I can't wait to be the one to tell him."

We rode in silence toward the palace. The quiet gave me a moment to wonder about what the future held for my brother—if he'd really be safe, if he'd be happy, and if he'd grow strong again.

I hoped so. And I hoped that the next time we met, it wasn't on opposing sides of a battlefront.

Dallas sat ramrod straight in front of me, his broad shoulders drawn back, lost in his own thoughts.

"Will you go back to Fifteen with Blake tonight?" I asked, as we got closer to the castle.

"No. We've quite run out of time. I saw Mira this afternoon—I told her to wrap up filming. I can't bear to pretend anymore."

"To pretend what?"

He chuckled, pulling me closer. "That there's actually a contest."

"Dallas!" A figure strode toward us, coming from the

palace. It was still light enough for me to make him out—tall, strapping, with closely cropped hair and an unmistakeable swagger. *Austin.*

"What news have you, brother?" Dallas called.

"Well, I held them off for as long as I could. I even had to dance with Lady Carlisle, so you owe me. I took one for the team." He grimaced.

"And?" Dallas asked.

"*And* to say that Father's pissed—well, it's the bloody understatement of the year." He reached us, and we stopped the horses and climbed down. Austin patted Maeve's mane and took her reins from Eve. He led the mare toward the castle. "There was a bit of a riot when the sentinels said they couldn't find you or the prisoner. But Father figured out what you were up to soon enough, and he pretended the whole thing had been his idea. He said he'd sent you off, to plant the rebel as a spy for us, and that the ceremony had been to give cover."

"Did the court believe him?"

Austin grunted. "They're a bunch of inbreeds, so probably. But Mother didn't buy it for a moment. I daresay she was pleased."

Dallas chuckled. "She's pretty pissed at him, so you're probably right."

"Listen, Mira Kinney and Tariq were just nipping at my heels," Austin said. "They want you and Gwyn to film your final date, or some bloody nonsense. They're waiting for you, ready to pounce."

"A bit ridiculous, don't you think, with everything else that's going on?" Eve asked.

"It is. They call it 'reality television' but really, it's nonsense..." Dallas scrubbed a hand over his face. "Still, the show must go on, I suppose. We have to finish what we started. But Mira and Tariq will have to wait. We have to see my father first."

We reached the castle and Eve took the reins back from Austin. "I'll bring the horses to the stable. I don't need to intrude on your family's privacy."

"You mean you want to avoid our family drama—and I don't blame you one bit." We climbed off our horse and Dallas bowed to her. "Thank you again, Eve. You've proven yourself a loyal member of the court, time and again. You have my loyalty in return."

She nodded. "Thank you, Your Highness." She would never admit to it, but I could hear the note of pride in her voice.

Austin watched her lead the horses away. "That's the one Mom turned, isn't it?"

"Yes." Dallas nodded. "She's actually become a fine vampire. You should see her fight."

Austin shook his head. "You've all gone a bit crazy down here. All this human contact, I don't know..." His gaze traveled over to me. "Speaking of humans. Will you forgive me, my lady?"

"For what?"

He arched an eyebrow. "For my attempt to scare you away from my brother?"

Dallas stepped forward. "What did you do?" he growled.

"Nothing. He was trying to give me a different

perspective, is all." I nodded to Austin as I grabbed Dallas's hand. "You needn't apologize. I appreciate that you're looking out for your brother, and in any event, you didn't scare me away."

Dallas started toward the castle again. "Let's go see my parents. Austin, you're coming, too. We've quite a bit of family business to take care of."

I cleared my throat. "Um, as I'm not technically family, I—"

"Are coming with us. I'm not letting you out of my sight again. Not ever." Dallas pulled me against him protectively.

Austin's gaze flicked between us. "You too are a bit much."

"Deal with it. And back me up with Father, or I'll see you banished from the North. I'll make you move down here to deal with him every day, like I have to."

Austin held up his hands in surrender. "I'll support you, I'll support you."

But I wondered, as we walked quickly through the courtyard and back inside the castle, if Austin's support would be enough. Dallas seemed certain of his position, and also, that he could protect me.

But what if he was wrong?

CHAPTER 24
YOU I CAN'T LIVE WITHOUT

MY HEART THUNDERED IN MY CHEST AS WE HEADED TO the throne room. "Don't be afraid," Dallas whispered, as we paused outside. "No one is ever going to hurt you again."

I nodded, trying to hide the fact that my insides were trembling. *Was that axe still within the king's reach?* But I exhaled in relief as we went through the doors—the weapons were gone, as was the red-hued Oriental rug.

But I stopped counting my blessings as soon as I faced the king. He sat on his throne, stone-faced, hands clenched so tightly around the armrests his knuckles glared white. Too afraid to even glance at Dallas, I stiffly curtsied, then waited—even though I wanted to run, screaming, away from the throne room forever.

The queen stood and nodded to the sentinels in the room. "Leave us."

As soon as they'd left and closed the door behind them, she bowed slightly. "Forgive the king. He seems to be at a loss for words. And manners, for that matter." She sank back down in her throne. "I see you've lost someone. Is he still alive, your brother?" She turned her sapphire gaze to me.

"Y-yes, Your Majesty. My brother lives."

"That's a blessing. I imagine he did not want to be changed."

I nodded jerkily, heart still pounding in my chest. "Thank you for sparing him." I doubted this was the right thing to say, but I blurted it out none the less.

"You needn't thank me—thank my sons. But I agree with their decision, even as my husband does not. I've learned from what happened with Eve. Changing her was a mistake, although I don't regret it, as she's become a valuable member of our court. But your brother never wanted this life. I believe we have a duty to respect that choice. I've learned—I'm still learning." The ghost of a smile whispered across her lips. "My sons are teaching me how to live in this new world. Who would have thought? I've raised them into fine young men, and now it is they who teach their mother."

Dallas and Austin bowed to her. Then Dallas turned to his father, who sat too still, his whole body coiled with obvious fury. "I know you do not approve of my actions."

"They are...treasonous." The king spat the words out.

"I am loyal to the woman I love, Father. She's my family as much as you are. It's my duty to protect her and her family."

"You would see this human, this rebel-lover, undo

everything that we've fought for?" the king cried, rising to his feet.

Dallas took a step forward. "You don't see the future the way that I do, Father. What we've fought for—these settlements—are ours to protect. Not to plunder—to *protect*. The rebels are a part of the settlement's past, present, and future. We've got to find a way to make common ground."

"Letting that traitor go back to his army solves nothing!"

"It solves something—it makes us look human, when we are not." Dallas's voice was calm and firm. "We must learn to show mercy, Father. We must show empathy, and in order to do that, we have to understand where the rebels are coming from, and what they fight for."

"They fight to take back their lands! And you've *handed* them a win!"

"I did no such thing. I let one of their members go free, instead of sentencing him to death. That's clemency, not cowardice. The sooner they understand that we want the same things they do—peace and prosperity for the settlements—they won't fear us so much. No matter what race we are."

The king rocked back on his heels. "You are too optimistic, son. You think that things can change. But I've lived long enough to know they cannot."

"But you're wrong. You are blind to the possibilities of the future. Gwyneth and I will rule these lands, someday. Human and vampire, together. And with your blessing, we will work to make them stronger, to make sure that every citizen has what they need, and grows to feel proud of their nation once more. So no, I would not see 'this human' undo everything we have fought for. I would see her as princess, and watch her bring the settlements into a prosperous, united future." He clasped my hand. "And I will have your word, Father, that you will never put her in harm's way again. Nor speak another ill word —to her face or about her. Her family—*all* of her family —is to have our protection, rebel or not."

The king took his son's measure. "And what if I decline? Such civilities aren't really in my nature, you know."

"Then you're a fool," Austin interjected. "The settlers love Dallas, Father. They'd merrily put a stake in your heart if it meant they got to wear T-shirts with Gwyn and Dallas on them, embellished with hearts and flowers, and got to watch their wedding on TV."

The king glowered at his younger son. "As I said earlier, you haven't been missed."

Austin smiled at his father. "Your pig-headedness will be your undoing. That's what we all say about you, behind your back."

The queen shot Austin a look. "That's quite enough, dear. Husband, there's some truth to what Austin says —not the pig-headed part, of course." The smile she gave the king said otherwise. "The polls have shown that both Gwyneth and Dallas are hugely popular with the people. The nation is rooting for them to get married. Their cumulative effect's been quite positive, which I might remind you is exactly what *you* wanted.

You've won, dear. The settlers are excited, and they're finally accepting the royal family as rulers. So let this come to its natural conclusion—a *triumph*. I know you're upset about the rebel, but let it go. Your son is in love. He has to do what's right for Gwyneth. I, for one, am proud to see him stand up for what he believes in."

"That's because you baby him, and you always have!" the king thundered.

"Right." Austin turned to us. "I think that's our cue to leave."

"Not just yet." Dallas stepped closer to his parents. "Father. *Father*."

The king stopped yelling long enough to look at his son.

"The competition is coming to an end. The Finale will be filmed tomorrow night. I need to know...can I count on you both? Will you give us your blessing, even after everything that's happened?"

The king took a deep breath. He looked to the queen, who nodded, then turned back to face Dallas. "I do not want to lose my son. I will support you, and I will support your choice. You have my word, even after everything that's happened."

Dallas bowed, then his gaze sought his mother's. "And you?"

The queen descended the steps. She kissed both of Dallas's cheeks. Then she turned to me, and took my hands in her icy ones. It was an odd feeling, having her so close. "I told you that I believed in fate. That's what brought you here, to my son." She nodded and released me.

Once she walked away, I resumed breathing.

"Then Mother, Father, we will take our leave. Thank you for your support and understanding." Dallas clasped my hand and smiling, led me from the throne room. Austin followed close behind.

I waited to speak until we were outside. "What does all that mean?" I asked, chest heaving.

Austin shrugged. "It means you're good to go."

I looked from Dallas to Austin, and back again. "So your father won't...you know...have my head on a spike?"

"Never." Dallas threw his arm around me as we headed toward the grand foyer.

"You're quite jovial," I noticed. I still didn't feel anywhere near relaxed.

"I am. I believe I just won." He grinned. "It feels good."

But the celebratory mood was cut short—Tamara, Shaye and Blake were in the hall with Mira Kinney and Tariq. All of them stared at us. Tamara's face flamed as she took in Dallas's arm thrown causally over my shoulder.

Tamara stepped closer, chest heaving. "What the... how dare you...this isn't fair..." she stammered, growing redder by the second, pointing in our direction. "You're supposed to be on a date with Blake!" She finally spluttered.

Dallas smiled at her patiently. "Hello, Miss Layne."

Tamara's jaw dropped in indignation. She turned to

Mira Kinney and Tariq. "I demand...I demand *something*. Some sort of justice. A rematch—or better yet, my final private date. Yes, I would like that." She crossed her arms against her chest, making sure her bosom protruded attractively. "I would like my date *now*." She used a tone that clearly indicated she planned to have her way.

"Actually, we have to speed the production up. The final dates have been cut from the schedule, except for His Highness and Miss West. They'll have their final date tonight." Mira Kinney's lightning-white smile flashed at Tamara.

I groaned. "Really? Do we have to?"

"Way to make my brother feel wanted," Austin joked.

"It's been a long day. I'm a bit exhausted, is all." I rubbed my neck, still thinking of that axe. "You vampires are a dramatic lot."

Dallas pulled me closer. "We don't have to do anything you don't want to."

Tamara watched us with unmasked fury. "Well, I *never*—"

"Sure you have," Blake teased. She got closer to Tamara and linked her arm through hers. "It's all right. I've been telling you for weeks that he loves Gwyn. You just don't like to listen to news that doesn't fit your—what's that you call it? The thing that 'represents' you?"

Tamara grimaced. "My brand."

"That's it. Your *brand*. Losing isn't your brand, as you said." Blake patted her arm, trying to console her.

"No one here will lose." Dallas released me and stepped forward. "In fact, I was hoping to ask a favor."

Tamara sniffed. "Good bloody luck."

He bowed to them. "Each of you have special qualities and unique gifts. The people have rallied around you because you are the best of what our nation has to offer. With you, the settlements can have a brighter future. The competition is almost over, but I was hoping to ask each of you to stay on. I'd like to offer you positions with my court, as Goodwill Ambassadors to the settlements."

Tamara seemed to perk up a bit. "Would we have actual titles?"

"Yes, of course. You'll be part of the royal court. You *must* have a title."

Tamara looked thoughtful. "Ambassador Layne... hmmm, it does have a certain ring to it, doesn't it?"

Dallas's eyes sparkled. "I was so impressed by your success tutoring the children, Miss Layne, I was hoping you'd have a special role working with underprivileged youth."

"You didn't think I actually *liked* working with children, did you?" Tamara scoffed. "I rather did that just for how it sounded on my resume."

"Of course." Dallas coughed. "In any event, the three of you—please consider my offer. You can give me your answer tomorrow night at the finale."

Austin cleared his throat. "We could probably use a Goodwill Ambassador up North."

Dallas turned to him, scowling. "For what purpose?"

Austin shrugged. "The North needs attention too, you know. If we're ever going to restore it to its former glory."

"You have plans to restore it to its former glory?"

"I've all sorts of plans that you know nothing about."

"We'll talk of this later." Dallas turned back to the others. "If you will excuse us, I should get Gwyneth to dinner before she falls asleep."

Mira Kinney stepped forward. "Gwyneth, please come with me. You have a twig in your hair and your makeup needs to be refreshed. Your Highness, I'll deliver her to you shortly. You're dining in the winter garden?"

"Correct."

"I'll have the camera crew ready." Mira held out her hand for me.

Dallas nodded to Austin and they stalked off together, talking in low tones.

I headed for Mira but stopped when I reached the other three girls. "Just a moment," I told the television host. I turned to Shaye and hugged her.

"What's that for?" she laughed.

"I haven't even seen you since you've been back. I'm sorry if this"—I nodded toward the hall where Dallas had just disappeared—"is all a bit of a shock. It just...we just...happened."

She clasped my hands, her eyes bright. "I've known for weeks that you two were in love. It's plain as day on both your faces. I didn't say anything because, well... Because I was still hoping, deep down, that I had a chance. But I've known the truth for a long time. And I couldn't be happier for you."

"Oh Shaye, thank you." Overcome with emotion, I

wiped my eyes. "Will you consider staying on as an ambassador? I'm not nearly ready to say goodbye."

"Of course I will! I'm thrilled to be asked, it's an honor!"

We hugged again and I turned to Tamara. "Tamara, I'm...I'm sorry that this didn't work out the way you'd hoped." She'd had every indication that things would, as usual, go her way. "If it's any consolation, my money's been on you this whole time. You're a winner, through and through. I've been petrified of you for weeks, cursing your name every chance I got."

"Well...good. I'm glad to hear it." Tamara shrugged prettily. "For the record, I never really wanted to marry the prince. So you're welcome to my sloppy seconds."

Blake snorted. "Tamara—"

"No, really. All I was after was a title. And I daresay I've got one." Tamara stuck her nose in the air. "*Ambassador Layne.* Yes, I've already quite gotten used to the sound of that. Now I just need some subservients to order around..."

I giggled and turned to Blake, pulling her aside for a moment. "Why do I feel like Austin just nominated you to be Ambassador to the North?"

"Right? It quite gave me the shivers!" Blake wrinkled her nose. "But I wonder if there's any food up there? It doesn't sound like the most welcoming place."

I squeezed my friend's hand. "We'll find out everything, and make sure it's all perfect. Don't worry."

Blake winked. "You know me. I never worry too much."

Feeling better, I let Mira lead me up the stairs. I had another dinner to get ready for, and what felt like miles to go before I could sleep.

❧

"You look lovely, Gwyneth."

"Thank you." I stifled a yawn as I picked at my roast chicken. "This is delicious. Thank you so much for an amazing night."

"It's my pleasure." Dallas chuckled and leaned forward. "Hopefully we won't put the audience to sleep with this performance. But really, you need to rest. You look like you're about to pass out in your mashed potatoes."

I nodded, feeling my eyelids droop. "But it's the winter garden, where we had our first date. I hate to waste the moment." I gazed around the room, still awed by how beautiful it was. The enormous windows showed all the stars, winking in the ever-darkening sky. Fairy lights lit up the garden around us.

He reached for my hand and squeezed it. "We'll have dinner here again, I promise. Let me take you to bed."

"Okay." I couldn't even pretend to argue.

Dallas nodded to the camera crew surrounding us. "We're done for the evening. I'm taking Miss West to bed." To my surprise, he swept me into his arms and picked me up, cradling me against his chest.

"You don't have to carry me." I giggled.

"You look like you might not make it." His voice

turned husky. "And after what my family put you through today... Let's just say I owe you one."

"You owe me nothing. And yet, when I am with you, I have everything."

He grinned at me, dark eyes sparkling as the camera crew scrambled to follow us up the stairs. When we reached my chambers he turned to them. "Go away," he growled. "We'll see you in the morning."

They bowed and scurried away, much to my delight. I arched an eyebrow at the prince. "Are you coming in for a sleepover?"

"If I'm invited."

"You have a standing invitation, Your Dallas."

He kicked the door open, grinning from ear to ear. "That's all I can ask for."

CHAPTER 25
THE FINALE

THERE WAS POUNDING ON MY DOOR AND I CURSED AS I sat up in bed—I'd fallen asleep without even kissing the prince!

Dallas was already at the door. "Yes, I'm coming. What the bloody hell is it? It's barely dawn!"

He opened the door and Evangeline stood there, her face white with shock. "Your Highness!" She fumbled through a curtsy. When she rose, she looked wildly from me in the bed to the prince, who was still buttoning his shirt. "I'm so sorry to interrupt!"

"You didn't interrupt anything, Evangeline." Dallas's voice turned gentle. "Miss West fell asleep during our date last night, and I stayed to watch over her."

I hopped out of bed so that poor Evangeline could see that I still wore my gown from the evening before. "Please don't be scandalized," I begged. "I can assure you that I fell asleep before I even got to properly thank His Highness with a goodnight kiss."

Evangeline blushed. "I'm not scandalized. Just a bit taken aback." She recovered and nodded to us urgently. "You must both come with me at once. I'm told that there's a stranger on the front steps—the sentinels said you should come quickly."

Dallas's eyes flashed. "Gwyneth, stay here."

Evangeline curtsied again. "I'm sorry, Your Highness —but they've asked for Miss West, too."

Perplexed, I grabbed Dallas's hand. We hurried downstairs, through the grand foyer and to the stairs that led to the palace entrance.

And what I saw there stopped my heart.

A man, pale and thin, lay sprawled out on the landing. He wore pauper's clothing. His cheeks were sunken and his hair had turned gray, but I would recognize him anywhere. "Father!"

I ran and threw myself to my knees, clutching his hand. "Daddy? Can you hear me?"

He opened his gray-green eyes and after a moment, he smiled. "Gwyneth. It's true. As I live and breathe, it's true." He lay back, clearly exhausted by the effort, but with the smile still on his face.

"We found this with him." One of the many sentinels guarding my father handed Dallas a note. He read it, then handed it to me.

Dear Gwyneth,
I returned to find Father in much worse condition. I feared that he would not last much longer. But now that I've seen the sort of resources that are available at the palace, I hoped you could

help him.

I am throwing myself—and our father—at the mercy of the royals. I pray that your prince was correct, and that your position there is secure. I also pray that you are safe, and that you can help our father.

I promised Dallas that I would never reveal anything I'd learned about the royals, and I intend to keep that promise. In return, he promised to protect you. I brought Father to the palace under cover of darkness. A soldier I trust with my life accompanied us, no one else. You have my word that this is no trick. Our father is no spy. His dying wish was to see you and the rest of our family again, and I refused to let my former prejudices stand in the way of that wish.

I hope you can help him. If not, at least he got to see his eldest daughter again, and see her happy.

I know you didn't want me to apologize, but I must. I am sorry for the terrible things I said to you. I am sorry that my hate blinded me. I am starting to see again, and the world looks different to me with these new eyes.

I didn't have the chance to say it to you before, but I wish you and your prince every happiness.

We'll see each other again someday. Even if it's on the other side, I'm looking forward to it.

Your Loving Brother,
Balkyn

"WILL HE RECOVER?" BETTINA ASKED, AS SHE PUT THE final touches on my makeup.

"I hope so. The prince has the best doctors attending to him."

Bria smoothed my hair, arranging the waves down my back. "It's amazing, isn't it? That you've been reunited with your father, after all these years!"

"It *is* amazing. I feel so blessed." My eyes filled with tears for the hundredth time that day. I'd spent the morning with my father, holding his hand as he floated in and out of consciousness. The doctors asked me to leave the medical ward in the early afternoon so that he could rest. But I was still overcome with emotion, thrilled to be near my father again. I'd immediately sent a letter to my mother. I didn't get into any of the specifics, just that Father was alive and being cared for at the palace.

"There, there—don't cry and make your mascara run," Bettina clucked. "Everything's going to be all right, I reckon."

"Y-yes."

Evangeline bustled in. "They're ready for you, Miss. Let's have a look at that gorgeous dress."

I stood up and teetered toward the full-length mirror. I would *never* get used to walking in high heels.

"Oh Miss." Evangeline put a hand over her heart. "You're stunning. That color pink suits you perfectly."

"Thank you. You ladies always make me look my best." I smiled at my reflection, admiring the rose silk of my halter-style dress.

"I daresay His Highness will approve. It really shows off your curves." Bria winked at me.

Bettina *tsked* at her twin, then turned to me, grinning.

"Tonight's the night. You'll be chosen as the princess—I just know it. And to think, your father will be here for the wedding! What a blessing!"

I held out my arms to them. "Can we have a group hug? I can't ever thank you enough for all you've done for me since I've been here. You're my second family." I sniffled, tears threatening again.

My maids hugged me but as soon as they pulled away, Bria swatted me. "Do *not* ruin your face. No more tears."

I nodded, deciding keeping my mouth shut was my best course of action—I really was quite close to blubbering.

Finally, it was time to go. I took deep, steadying breaths as I headed for the ballroom. *Not much longer, now.* Still, I had to clutch the wall for support by the time I made it down the hall.

This was it.

The ballroom was decorated elegantly, with fresh flowers in crystal vases and thousands of flickering candles. Mira Kinney was stunning in a gold brocade ballgown. She was busy barking orders at Rose, her assistant, as well as the rest of the production crew. There were cameras everywhere, which of course did nothing for the knocking of my knees and the pounding of my heart.

The king and queen sat slightly removed from the activity, their thrones atop the stone dais. I made a beeline for them; it was best to get this over with. But Tariq stepped into my path, bowing with a flourish. "My Lady. A word, if you will."

Bloody hell. "Of course, Tariq."

He fluttered his long, thick lashes at me. "As I understand it, tonight will be a victory lap for you."

"We'll see, I suppose."

He stepped closer, his expensive cologne wafting over me, making my nose itch. "I'm afraid you and I never really got off on the right foot. I just wanted to apologize for anything in my behavior that may have offended over the past weeks."

I resisted the urge to scratch my nose. "It's a bit late for that, don't you think?"

"I hope not." He sounded sincere, and really, a bit hopeless.

I smiled at him. "I'm not one to hold grudges, Tariq." His oily smile appeared so quickly, it made me regret my easy forgiveness. "But if I were you, I'd make sure to stay on the prince's good side. He does have a bit of a temper, you know."

He cleared his throat as he bowed deferentially. "Yes, my lady."

"If you'll excuse me." *If you'll excuse me, I have to go and see my future in-laws, one of whom would love it if the earth suddenly swallowed me whole. Or worse.*

I nervously approached the king and queen, my heart in my throat. I curtsied, keeping myself as steady as I could. "Your Majesties. I just wanted to say—I just wanted to say thank you." Tears sprung to my eyes again. "Dallas told me that you gave permission for my father to receive medical treatment. I do not know what to say. Your generosity and kindness, your willingness to forgive...it's all left me a bit speechless, I'm afraid." I bowed my head, embarrassed and still on the verge of tears.

"Child please, look at me." The queen's unusual voice, once foreign to me, soothed my nerves. I looked up. "We are happy to have your father here, just as we are thrilled to be a part of this evening. Our son has found true happiness, something you always worry about as a parent. As he chooses you, we choose you. We welcome you into our family with an open heart."

"T-thank you, Your Majesty." Boy, I really hoped the prince picked me. This would all be quite embarrassing otherwise.

"We offer our congratulations," the king said stiffly.

As I really couldn't expect more than that, I curtsied again and hurried off.

Blake was, of course, stationed next to the hors d'oeuvres.

"You look lovely." I hugged her, careful of her tightly fitted black gown.

"Thank you. This dress is a bit squeeze-y, though." She tugged on it. "I hope it doesn't interfere with my plans to eat myself silly."

"When Dallas asks you about staying on as an ambassador, what will you say?" I couldn't bear to say goodbye to my friend.

"I'll say yes, of course. I'd like to do something useful with my life. And I like the sound of the title, too: Ambassador Kensington. It's quite posh."

I grinned at her. "It suits you."

Austin sauntered over, looking quite posh himself in a dark-grey ceremonial uniform, a deep-purple cape sailing out behind him. "Miss Kensington, have you had a moment to think about what we discussed?"

I looked quickly at Blake. "You've discussed something?"

She nearly choked on her canapé. "A bit." She turned back to Austin. "I need more details, I'm afraid. I want to hear about these bloody gnomes. And what your kitchen staff is like."

Shaye and Tamara waved me over, and I reluctantly stopped eavesdropping on Blake and Austin's conversation. "What's going on with those two?" Shaye asked, excited.

"Something, but I'm not sure what." I gasped as I focused on her. "Shaye, you look stunning!"

She grinned, smoothing her gown, the color of fresh spring grass. "My maids outdid themselves. I'm going to miss them so much."

"You won't have to." Tamara shrugged. "Ambassadors get to keep their maids. I already negotiated that."

I laughed, but I shouldn't have been surprised. "You already negotiated the terms of your appointment?"

"'Course I did." Tamara shrugged, showing off her toned shoulders in her gorgeous, deep-purple strapless gown. "I don't take these things lightly."

"Nor should you." I hugged them both. "I'm so glad you're both staying on."

"Don't be so dramatic." Tamara brushed me off, but I could tell she was pleased. "If I wasn't becoming an ambassador, I'd be becoming the princess. There was no way I was going back to civilian life. I was meant to be part of the royal court; I've always known that."

Since there was no use arguing with her, I chuckled instead. But then I spotted Eve in the corner. She looked as if she were wrestling with her floor-length, floral gown. "Excuse me for a moment." I hustled to my friend, who looked distressed. "What's the matter?"

"It's just this dress. It's a bit bustle-y, is all." Eve groaned as she tried to fluff the skirts. "My kingdom for a tunic and a pair of pants."

"There, there, let me help you." I smoothed her skirts and arranged them so they fell to the floor just right. I grinned at her. "You look beautiful, Eve."

"You don't have to be so chuffed about it. I'd rather be fighting someone with my stick."

I giggled, linking my arm through hers, leading her to the others. "It's just one night."

"And then we have the bloody wedding—"

"Speaking of. If I'm chosen by the prince, would you do me the honor of being my maid of honor?"

"Of course you're going to be chosen by the prince, stop being so ridiculous!" She stuck her chin up, curls bouncing. "And as for that other business you mentioned...I'd be honored." She would never admit it, but I could tell she was pleased.

"I'm the one who's honored."

We joined the others and Mira Kinney took center stage, surrounded by cameras, her gold gown glinting under the klieg lights. "Thank you all for being here.

What a whirlwind!" She laughed as we all politely clapped. "Without further ado, I'd like to introduce His Royal Highness, Prince Dallas Black, Crown Prince of the United Settlements—the reason we're all here!"

Trumpets sounded as the prince strode through the double doors, his ebony cape sailing out behind him. My heart leapt into my throat as he came closer and I could see his broad chest, handsome face, and thick, luxurious hair.

It just never got old. I fanned myself, staring.

He grinned when he reached Mira, taking her hand and kissing it. Then he swept into a deep bow. He smiled when he raised himself back up, his gaze finding mine.

"Have you made your choice, Your Highness?"

"Yes, Mira, I have." He stepped forward and the cameras swarmed around him, getting every angle. "But first of all, I'd be remiss if I didn't thank some very important people. My parents, the king and queen, for sponsoring this competition and supporting me at every turn. I salute you." He bowed to his parents, who nodded in return. "I must thank my brother, Austin Black, for coming to my aid when I needed him most."

Grinning, Austin and Dallas bowed to each other.

"I would also like to thank the finalists, and their families, for participating in this contest. It hasn't been for the faint of heart, let me tell you." He chuckled. "Thank you also to Mira Kinney and her crew, for making this almost painless. Almost."

He took a moment, and then cleared his throat. "I found it too difficult to let each of these young women go. Every one of them is talented, special, and each of them have something to give back to our great nation. So I will ask the three contestants I am not proposing to this evening if they would like to stay on as members of the royal court. I ask each of them to become Goodwill Ambassadors, to continue with outreach on behalf of the royal family. I will start with these fine young women."

Tariq came and lined us up. Me, Blake, Shaye and Tamara, in a row in front of the prince.

"Miss Shaye Iman, would you accept the position of Goodwill Ambassador? Will you continue your good work with the settlements on behalf of the royal family?"

Shaye grinned at him and stepped forward. "I'm honored, Your Highness. I accept."

Dallas hugged her, smiling. "Thank you." Shaye went to stand off to the side, and Dallas faced us again. "Miss Tamara Layne. Will you accept the position of Goodwill Ambassador, and continue your good work with the settlements on behalf of the royal family?"

Tamara smiled a positively royal smile as she stepped forward. "Of course, Your Highness. It is my honor to continue to serve the royal court, and to become an integral member."

Dallas hugged her and thanked her. Tamara went next to Shaye, standing with her hand on her hips for the best photographic effect.

"Miss Blake Kensington. Would you accept the position as a Goodwill Ambassador to the North? Will you continue your good work on behalf of the royal settlements in our northern counterpart?"

Austin was staring hard at Blake, a fact that did not go unnoticed by her. Blushing, she stepped forward. "I do accept, Your Highness. And may I also add something?"

Dallas smiled at her. "Of course."

Blake grinned. "I wish you every happiness." She hustled next to Tamara and Shaye, happy to be out of the spotlight.

Dallas cleared his throat. Did I imagine it, or did he look a bit nervous? "Miss West, that leaves you."

I smiled at him. "Well... I suppose it does."

"Miss West, in you, I have found a partner to complete me. I have found a friend, a confidant, someone who understands me as no one else can. I have found hope, courage, and a vision of the future that I never had before. You make me...you make me whole, Gwyneth. I didn't realize how alone I'd been until you came into my life."

"Oh." I wiped at my eyes. "Quite."

Seeing how moved I was, Dallas grinned. Then he got down on one knee. He took a dark-satin box from his pocket, then opened it to reveal an enormous, emerald-cut diamond in an antique platinum setting.

My heart thudded in the best sort of way.

"Miss West—My Gwyneth... Will you marry me?"

There was only one answer. I reached for his hand, knowing I would never let it go again. "Yes."

AFTERWORD

Thank you so much for reading this book! It means everything to me! The next book is coming soon!

If you enjoyed *The Finale*, **please** consider leaving a review on Amazon! Short or long, reviews help other readers find books they'll enjoy. It doesn't have to be fancy—just a few quick words that you enjoyed the book!

This is a brand-new series, so your review means a lot! Thank you so much for considering it!

The next book is coming soon! You can subscribe to my newsletter for new-release notifications:

www.leighwalkerbooks.com

Thank you again. It is THRILLING for me to have you read my book. Please sign up for my newsletter and come along for the exciting adventures with the Vampire Royals!

xxoo

Leigh Walker

ALSO BY LEIGH WALKER

Vampire Royals

The Pageant (Book #1)

The Gala (Book #2)

The Finale (Book #3)

The North (Book #4 — Coming Soon!)

The Division Series

Premonition (Book #1)

Intuition (Book #2)

Perception (Book #3)

Divination (Book #4)

ABOUT THE AUTHOR

Leigh Walker lives in New Hampshire with her husband and three adorable, brilliant, talented children who play almost every sport on the planet and help clean the house only when direct threats are issued.

In her pre-author life, Leigh had many different jobs. She worked in advertising at *Boston Magazine* and was a copy editor at *Chadwick's*, the women's fashion catalog. She was also a barback, waitress, barista, receptionist, and lawyer. She loves being a full-time writer and sports-mom best.

Outside of writing and family, her priorities include maintaining a sense of humor, caffeine, chocolate, *Grey's Anatomy*, *Westworld*, and Chris Rock's *Tamborine*.

She loves to hear from readers! Email her at leigh@leighwalkerbooks.com, and sign up for her mailing list at www.leighwalkerbooks.com.

www.leighwalkerbooks.com
leigh@leighwalkerbooks.com

ACKNOWLEDGMENTS

Thank you to my readers for joining me! Your support means everything. Readers for the win!

This series is so much fun to write. I love Gwyneth and Dallas and, of course, Shaye, Blake, and Tamara. Yes, I love Tamara. She's always fun to write. I feel as if she's going to jump off the page and start causing trouble!

Speaking of love, I must give love to my family, who put up with my blank stares, my crazy ideas, and me in general. A special shout-out to my kids, who always have my back and make me smile. Love, love, love you. Love for the win!

Speaking of my kids, my 11-year old tells me that I listen to "old people music." At some point I will ground him for this, but in the interim, I have to thank the band U2—who he insists falls into this category—for the song "Red Hill Mining Town." I listened to that song about a thousand times writing this book, and a lot of the lyrics turned into chapter titles. Bono for the win!

Thanks to my mom, who always supports and helps me. She loves Dallas almost as much as I do. Love you, Mom. Moms for the win!

I also want to thank my editors at Red Adept Editing. They edit all my independently published books, and I love working with them. They're the best. It's so nice to have a team, even when I'm a free agent!

The next book is coming soon! I can't wait to share it with you!

That's a lot of exclamation points in a few short paragraphs, lol. But this book world gets me excited, and so does the fact that you're coming along for the ride. I'm signing off to write now, but just so you know, I am, forever and truly, **#teamdallas.**

See you in the next book!

xoxo

Leigh

PS: Sign up for my mailing list at www.leighwalkerbooks.com so you know when the next book comes out!

Made in the USA
San Bernardino, CA
01 April 2019